ULTIM

ESBIAN EROTICA

ULTIMATE LESBIAN EROTICA

EDITED BY NICOLE FOSTER

2009

alyson books
NEW YORK

Manufactured in the United States of America

Published by Alyson Books
245 West 17th Street, New York, NY 10011

Distribution in the United Kingdom by
Turnaround Publisher Services Ltd.
Unit 3, Olympia Trading Estate, Coburg Road, Wood Green
London N22 6TZ England

First Edition: January 2009

09 10 11 12 13 14 15 16 17 18 a 10 9 8 7 6 5 4 3 2 1

ISBN-10: 1-59350-091-2
ISBN-13: 978-1-59350-091-7

Library of Congress Cataloging-in-Publication data are on file.

Cover design by Victor Mingovits

CONTENTS

INTRODUCTION

DESIRE. EVEN THE WORD itself is sexy—low and rumbling, charged with the barely restrained energy of our deepest yearnings. It's one of those feelings that our bodies understand better than our minds, making our hearts race and our muscles tense, readying us for whatever's next. The feeling of wanting someone is universal, and the women in this book get what they want. With the wide variety of lovers and locales, you're sure to get what you want, too.

How about a steamy afternoon on an (almost) deserted island? Or a road trip up north that turns into more than some lakeside lounging? Even a community service project can become the backdrop for a romantic rendezvous when two young women discover that helping the needy applies to themselves, as well.

But maybe you're looking for something a little less run-of-the-mill. A threesome with a porn star may be more to your liking, or a moonlit run-in with an amorous immortal. Perhaps you're longing to leave this world entirely and imagine the cosmic eroticism of a virgin goddess whose passions are awakened for the first time.

The women in these stories are as diverse as their readers, but they have one important quality in common: attitude. Shy or shameless, take heed or take-charge, they're willing to grope—literally—for satisfaction, and help their partners do the same. If you learn one thing from *Ultimate Lesbian Erotica 2009*, let it be the lesson of asking for what you want. You may just come away surprised.

—*Nicole Foster*

BEACH MOTH

GILL McKNIGHT

"YOU DAFT OLD fuck! Come back here, you stupid old bastard."

It was no good. Between the early evening breeze blowing her words back in her face, and the growl and burp of his antiquated engine, Chevral and his other twenty-seven passengers hadn't a chance of hearing her yelling. She watched aghast as the little ferry wobbled towards the western tip of Blimbing Bay before being swallowed by the glorious sunset. For one infinitesimal moment the small craft became an inky outline against a perfect circle of molten lava, shimmering on a diamante sea. Involuntarily her hand strayed to the camera bag slung at her side, then hesitated. Instead she screeched, "You're all a pack of wankers."

In utter disbelief she stood as her shipmates, and her one and only ride home, slid out of sight around the headland. The small craft happily bouncing back to the resort sans one. *None of those pissheads will notice I'm missing.*

They would all be facing that brilliant orange sunset, swilling beer, while she stood marooned on a beach in the arsehole of nowhere. Twenty-seven young people packed onto a boat, probably only licensed for eighteen, on their way back to the cosy resort complex for dinner and dancing.

"Hope they drown."

Now what? She couldn't believe she'd been forgotten. All she'd done was nip into the undergrowth for what—all of ten minutes? Hadn't Chevral himself told her where to go look for the birds?

Okay, so maybe she was a little longer than ten minutes, but those Yellow-crested Cockatoos were magnificent. She had seen two, and the photographer in her couldn't let the chance pass by. As a freelancer she needed something to offset the cost of this holiday, or at least justify it. Hopefully she might be able to sell the pictures to a bird-watching magazine back home. That would certainly help balance her expenses. The last thing she'd expected was to return to the beach and find her fellow beachcombers had left without her.

What the hell was she to do now? She knew nothing about this part of the island, except that it took over an hour of hell in Chevral's weaving, bobbing, fume-filled boat to get here. Long shadows crawled across the sand, alarming her. Night was falling rapidly. Scrabbling through her camera bag she searched for her cell phone. *Ah ha! Thank God I remembered it. Please let there be a signal.*

Flipping up the cover she squinted at the small screen. Damn it. No signal. She stood frozen, mesmerised by the darkening horizon as she wondered what to do. If she slept out on the beach the mozzies would eat her alive. And God knows what else—there could be Komodo dragons here for all she knew. Panic began to bubble, percolating away in her guts.

Just then, out of the corner of her eye, she saw it. Several meters back from the shoreline and to her right a light flickered on in a window. She almost laughed out loud in relief. There was a building back there. The pathway up from the beach was leafy and overgrown but totally obvious now that she saw the light shining down its length.

It has to be a beach bar. Right now she could murder a vodka and tonic with a ton of ice. Reshouldering her camera bag, she dumped her useless cell phone back in its depths and headed for the weak yellow haze.

Several yards along the path it became clear this was no bar. It was an old, beat-up joglo. Well, that's what she would call it, if she were in real estate trying to dump the rundown wreck on some hapless holidaymaker. It was obviously a private holiday home that used to be a traditional native dwelling. Probably some savvy islander had sold it to a halfwit tourist.

She slowed as she approached. The veranda was in shadows despite the weak light from the open window. Shifting her bag to the other shoulder, she tentatively placed a foot on the first step.

"Lost."

It was a statement, not a question, and came out of the darkness to her right. It startled her. Squinting she could make out the glow of a cigarette. A disembodied woman's voice floated somewhere above it.

"More like abandoned," she answered, not moving. Her eyes drilled the darkness for clues. A scrape of a chair leg on the planked floor, and then a footfall as her host politely moved forward into the meagre light.

A tall Westerner emerged from the gloom. Long, dark blonde hair swept across her shoulders, bright blue eyes over a broad smile. Her style was retro surfer chick, and she had the body to back it up. Sawn-off denims frayed mid thigh on long tanned legs. She was tall and her height was obviously all in her legs. A scrappy old T-shirt casually drooped from square shoulders. The soft cotton caught the curve of her chest.

"Chevral head back without ya, then?" Her smile was quirky as she took another hit of a joint, not a cigarette. Her drawl was American.

"Hi, name's Teena, by the way." She introduced herself as an afterthought, and then drifted back to the darkened corner and her chair. "Come and sit."

It seemed a civilized offer, and if it came with a hit she was happy to follow. No other options sprang to mind.

"Yeah. Guess I'm marooned for the night. I was starting to get a little freaked till I saw your light." She followed Teena and took a seat. "I'm Karrie. I'm staying at Neptune's Point."

A rickety table held an overflowing ashtray and all the paraphernalia for rolling jays. She was glad to see a bottle of dark rum; she could drink that in a pinch, though vodka would have been better. Even as she looked longingly at the bottle it was pushed across.

"Have a drink. Sorry, got no glasses. Well, no clean ones."

Shrugging Karrie lifted the neck to her lips and took a gulp. The red-hot liquid burned all the way down, turning her guts into a lava pit.

"Jesus," she wheezed, "that's rough." This was greeted with a deep laugh that had the same heated effect on her belly.

"Local hooch. You have to be in the know to score some. And believe me, there's no antidote; in the morning you suffer until you drink again."

"Perfect marketing." She took another swig to butch herself up. Another belly buzz warned that the drink was almost as potent as her host's pheromones. Both were making her head light and her blood pound nicely in all the wrong places.

"Here." The reefer was passed in a tight finger pinch; delicately she brushed her hand across warm tanned skin to collect it. The touch added to her tingles. A long draw, a big hit, and yes . . . *What a beautiful evening. Just look at the stars on the horizon, the way the tree fronds sway . . .*

"That's some shit." Appreciation shone in her husky voice. She cleared her throat.

"Yeah." They sat quietly for a long time watching the last of the evening melt away into night. The bottle, and another joint were swapped casually between them.

"What ya photograph?" Teena suddenly seemed chatty, nodding at the bag at Karrie's feet.

"Birds. Wildlife and stuff. Sell it to magazines. It's okay." All her sentences ran together. Teena giggled. Karrie snorted, "I'm smashed." Silence, then . . .

"Come here."

Karrie stood and moved with surprising fluidity. She had half expected to fall flat on her face. Teena reached out and guided her astride her lap. They sat, eyes locked, inches apart for several seconds, before Teena took the hem of Karrie's T-shirt and swept it up over her head, dropping it on the floor. The exposed breasts were high and round, with toffeed nipples peeking up at her invitingly. They puckered tightly in anticipation before Teena even touched them.

Teena's wide, generous mouth bent to suck on a chewy cocoa tip, drawing it in deep, before closing her teeth to nip around its base. Karrie arched up, almost rising off Teena's lap, pressing hard into her mouth. She hissed at the sting. As suddenly as it hurt, a soft tongue bathed the ache away with lazy, swirling strokes. Dragging across the sensitive bud, delightful and soothing; before sharp white teeth nipped again.

Her other breast was cupped and kneaded, strong fingers tugged on the nipple until it was fully erect, fitting snugly into the heart of Teena's palm. The soft tissue was lovingly circled and compressed. Teena took her time, flattening, kneading, pinching, moving back and forth from breast to breast, swapping mouth for hand, until Karrie's tits hummed with heat and sensation. She squirmed as the pressure and wetness between her thighs increased.

"C'mon," she whispered, "c'mon. Fuck me. Please. Yessss . . ." She hissed at yet another deliciously soft nip on her swollen nipples. They stood out hard and thick; she swore they were bigger than ever before. Teena broke away, a broad smile covering her face.

"Sure I will. Stand up. C'mon, up ya get." A steadying hand helped Karrie to her feet. She stood swaying as quick fingers unzipped her shorts. The button popped, and they fell around her ankles. She stepped out, kicking them away. Naked, she sat back down, straddling Teena's thighs. The taller woman spread hers, stretching Karrie wider, totally exposing her sex. Teena ran her hands up Karrie's shivering abdomen to cup her breasts again. She slipped each nipple into the fork between thumb and palm, squeezing the sensitive tips tightly then releasing them, delighting in Karrie's soft moans. A sex musk rose up between them, whetting Teena's appetite even more. She continued nipple squeezing until the air was thick with Karrie's horny scent and moans.

Karrie's hips rocked against nothing. She was spread open to the air alone, and she needed something hard against her, and in her, and soon. Her clit throbbed, big and plump and very discontent at being ignored. But she could fix that herself. She removed her hands from Teena's shoulders and trailed them down her own belly, intent on satisfying her clit's demands. At once her breasts were abandoned and Teena reached out to grab her wrists.

"Oh, no. That's my job."

Karrie's arms were pulled apart and she fell forward into Teena's hungry mouth. She was held cruciform as Teena roughly sucked her tits, until Karrie cried out with frustration and need. Teena pulled back, greedily observing the spit slicked breasts and the swollen nipples. She blew cool air across them, smiling as Karrie twitched.

"Hot, huh?" She smiled, letting Karrie's wrist go. "Turn round. Sit with your back to me." On shaking legs Karrie complied, her bottom snug against Teena's groin. It was obvious Teena was topping her, but Karrie was enjoying the game.

She leaned back, resting on Teena's shoulder as her hands were taken and placed over her own hot breasts. She moaned; they were tender, the tips overworked and sore. Teena's hands covered hers and roughly squashed the pliant flesh.

"Do they feel bigger?" she murmured into her ear. Karrie moaned and nodded. They were definitely swollen."Aren't you going to thank me for making your tits bigger?" The question hummed in her ear.

"Thank you." Silence, then the hands covering hers mashed her palms onto her stinging nipples, causing her to squeak.

"Thank you, Teena, for giving me such big tits." She hastily amended, learning quickly.

"You're welcome, Karrie," Teena whispered in response. As she spoke she spread her own thighs apart. Karrie's legs, hooked over hers, were spread too, her sex opened wide and her musk blooming into the night air. She was so turned on, so slick and wet. She knew she was being positioned for Teena's requirements, and this excited her even more.

"Show me how you rub your tits," Teena murmured again, her husky voice making Karrie's belly quiver. She moved her hands down to the splayed inner thighs and idly stroked as she watched Karrie rub her own breasts in small circles. Teena drew her blunt nails along the trembling flesh.

"Now pinch real tight." Her fingers began to brush against sodden curls. She smiled at Karrie's hiss as she squeezed the tender points. Tickling, Teena's fingertips lightly swirled in slick wetness.

"Is that real tight?" she questioned Karrie.

Groaning out loud, her hips undulating frantically against the teasing fingers, Karrie nodded in answer. "Uh huh."

"Oh?" Teena sounded dubious. "Pull on them for me. Right out. I want to see them stretched out between your finger and thumb. Let's get you some big, long nipples to go with them big tits, hmm?" She nipped a tanned shoulder and then licked at the crescent marks of her teeth. Whimpering with pain and excitement, Karrie pinched her nipples harder and pulled the protesting points out until they extended from her body as far as possible. Her entire breast lifted to follow. She mewled, her hips pumping air.

"Good girl. Take a treat." Two fingers slipped between Karrie's soaked folds. Her hips spasmed as the fingers pushed in deeper.

"God, you're so ready." Teena was a little surprised at the suction. She swirled her thumb across the fat clitoris. Karrie nearly leapt off her lap.

"You're much closer than I guessed." Teena was a little alarmed; she wanted to drag this first orgasm out longer. It was always the most delicious, most torturous. Quickly she withdrew her fingers.

"No." Karri sank back letting go of her aching breasts. "It's not fair. Stop teasing." She was becoming too frustrated and annoyed. The game wasn't fun anymore. She wanted to fuck. Teena ignored the protests and positioned her along her lap to perch on her knees.

"Shhh, I'll look after you. Bend over." She pushed Karrie forward, her hand in the small of her back. "More. That's right, all the way down. Put your palms flat on the floor."

She groaned in pleasure. Karrie was bent right over, facing away from her, her sex from anus to clit on full display and easily accessible to both Teena's hands. An inquisitive forefinger pushed against Karrie's puckered asshole. The girl jumped and cast an anxious glance over her shoulder.

"Don't worry." Teena smiled, and slid her hand down and across the sopping sex. With two fingers she began to fuck Karrie from behind in earnest. Karrie groaned and swung her hips into the rhythm. Teena increased the thrust and added another finger, spreading them a little, making sure Karrie felt full.

Karrie moaned and pushed back on the hand; using her palms as leverage she bounced on the rigid fingers impaling her. Her whole universe was centered on her cunt and what Teena was doing to it. Her inner muscles contracted tight, then rippled and flowed, one minute a band of iron, the next melting honey. The tropical night air was filled with the wet slap, and the small puffs and grunts of fucking.

Teena's palm was damp with Karrie's sex. She brought her free forefinger across and coated it. When it was lubricated, she pushed the tip against the puckered ass rolling before her. Karrie peeked over her shoulder on feeling this new sensation. Teena smiled gently.

"Relax. Let it happen. If your body wants it, it'll take it."

A look of trust flashed between them and Karrie returned her attention to rocking on Teena's fingers, and coming big time. The fingertip rimming her asshole felt nice.

Karrie's bouncing bottom put pressure on the fingertip, and it slid slowly inside her up to the first knuckle. She cried out in sighing pleasure. Teena held back, giving Karrie absolute control over the amount of penetration. The sensation of Teena's fingers in both passages was exquisite.

"I knew you'd like it," Teena breathed, admiring the luscious ass squirming before her. Now she took over and began a hard rhythm, synchronized between both holes. Karrie grunted and writhed; she was so close.

"Rub your clit," Teena ordered.

First touch and it exploded, breaking her into a million screaming pieces. White light crashed through her head as she jerked and spasmed. Sweat-drenched and exhausted, she felt arms enfold her. She was pulled up and across until she sat curled on Teena's lap in a massive, warm hug. Gentle lips nuzzled her ear.

"Was that okay?" Little kisses peppered her brow and cheek.

"God, I thought I was gonna die," she rasped, exhausted, and content. "Maybe Chevral did me a favor after all." Her dope, rum, and sex buzz were mellowing out nicely.

A crooning laugh floated in her ear as she cuddled in deeper. "No. He does me the favors. Always tries to leave me a nice girl, if he sees one."

Karrie's head whipped round. "You mean that stupid old goat and you have a deal?"

"Yeah. I'm out here working on my third novel. It gets lonely. Chevral tries to find me a . . . companion, from time to time. But it's hit or miss. *You* are a hit. A definite hit." She was squeezed possessively, and more kisses were dropped onto Karrie's neck and hair.

Karrie pushed away, sputtering indignantly. "I don't believe it. The nerve of you two. How the hell do I get back to the resort?"

Teena shrugged nonchalantly, but her face showed real disappointment. "He'll be back tomorrow. You can sleep in my bed until then. In fact, I'll go radio him now and get him to come at first light, okay?"

Reluctantly she stood, carefully setting Karrie onto her feet. As she moved away the photographer began to angrily drag on her shorts and T-shirt. How dare they trick her like that? It was nothing short of pimping! So what if she looked easy. She was on holiday—everyone was easy on vacation.

She followed Teena to the doorway. Leaning on the doorpost, she looked around the modest cabin. It was basic but cozy, kept clean and tidy. She stepped farther in. Teena was sitting at a desk that held a marine radio and her laptop. The American looked despondent as she halfheartedly pushed the buttons. For the first time Karrie noticed an air of loneliness about her. *It must be boring as hell out here. What good is an island paradise for one?*

Every move Karrie made, her nipples ached sweetly against her cotton top. Her cunt and ass felt equally happy. Her body was definitely trying to tell her something.

She looked at the lean, attractive blonde who had just fucked her senseless. She thought of the Yellow-crested Cockatoos in the greenery outside, and the other untold photographic opportunities on this quieter side of the island.

"Hey," she called over to the woman holding the radio handset. Teena glanced up, her eyes guarded, her look soft and dejected. "See if he can bring my bags."

"BLR"

K. SONTZ

"GOOD NIGHT, MIKEY," I WHISPERED, kissing his cheek.

"G'night, Jackie!" The little boy yawned and curled up with his stuffed duck. He was the picture of innocence—no one would suspect that it had taken over an hour to wrangle him into bed. The Mickey Mouse clock next to his bed read 9:30. I sighed and rubbed my strawberry blonde crewcut. It was way past this three-year-old's bedtime. At least an hour too early to go out and do anything exciting. Not that I could have any fun tonight, even if I wasn't trapped watching *Veggie Tales* with a whiny toddler—it was summer break, and I was stuck at home in Coeur d'Alene after my first year at the University of Washington. None of the internships I had applied for in Seattle had come through, so I was back babysitting again. Just like when I was thirteen and desperate to get out.

Well, not quite like when I was thirteen. Back then I used to put the kid to bed and spend the rest of the evening hanging out in the kitchen, doing homework. Math, or whatever. I was a good girl—I didn't care about anything besides getting the grades that could get me out of this town and into a good school. After I graduated with a 4.0 and headed west to the U-Dub, I found out that going to a good school meant that I didn't want to be a good girl anymore.

College turned out to be way more fun than I was expecting. Within a month I had joined the gay student union, started calling myself a lesbian ("dyke" if I wanted be shocking), and shaved my head. I started dating Lisa in April. It would have been tragic, hooking up so close to the end of the year, but by some coincidence (fate, I thought secretly) she was from a town not too far away from me, and would be spending the summer there as well. She worked for her dad's catering company, and I only took the babysitting gig tonight because she had to help him out at a job. We had made tentative plans to meet up after—drink coffee for hours at a nearby Denny's, maybe neck in the car—but who knew when the wedding she was working at was going to be over.

I plopped down onto the couch and pulled out a copy of *Beebo Brinker*. The GSU's president told me it was required reading if I was to call myself queer, but I wasn't sure how much I liked it. The atmosphere was kind of cool—the whole gay, bohemian subculture. It was really interesting, actually—the butch/femme thing, the secret codes, the way they had to create their own language for who they were and what they were doing. And yeah, I'm sure it was daring for its time. It kind of killed me, though, how they would talk about being gay but never got into the fucking. Honestly, that was why I preferred *The L Word*. I'd grunt and nod whenever some of the more radical dykes on campus would rag on about, like, the classism in the show or whatever. But I was the one who made five bucks an hour being tortured by a screaming child. Just thinking about Shane could make me feel better.

It wasn't exactly easy being a girl who liked girls in Idaho, though, even in the twenty-first century. When I went to visit the university with my parents, they asked the admissions representative what one of the silliest questions they ever got was. The student, a senior, a boy with stretched earlobes and a lip piercing, said, "Occasionally someone will ask, 'Will going to school in the city make my son or daughter gay?' " My parents laughed uncomfortably. So did I, but for different reasons. When I came back for Thanksgiving break with no hair my mom almost had a heart attack, and my dad didn't look me in the eye. They weren't going to kick me out or anything, but it was really clear that I wasn't to talk to them about anything I did at school aside from homework.

Lisa had it even worse. I went to meet her at a gig one time, and her dad saw me, in jeans and a yellow tank top with my shaved head. That night I got an e-mail from Lisa saying that she was practically under house arrest, for the offense of "bringing a bulldagger in front of the family." (Me, a bulldagger? I was wearing Hello Kitty earrings!). She said that they blamed me for turning her into a homosexual, which was ridiculous since she started having sex with girls when she was fifteen, and she was my first girlfriend. Lisa wasn't sure if her parents were going to let her go back to school in the fall. They were looking at local community colleges, ones that would let her live at home, but she was trying to convince them that she would find a therapist who would "cure" her in the city. She had promised them that she'd let herself try and be fixed, if only they would let her get her degree. I told her that if she had to she could run away and live with me, but she brushed me aside.

"I'll convince them," she said. "They don't like having me around any more than I like being around them. It'll be fine, babe, don't you worry."

One day Lisa told her parents that she was going to a doctor's appointment, and we met in a little artist's town far away. We took the risk of holding hands on the street. As a maroon SUV trundled past we heard a little boy's voice yell "Lesbos!" out the window. She got pissed, but I started to laugh.

"How observant!" I shouted at the passing car. Who uses the word "lesbo" anymore, really? Still, it was upsetting. I bet that kid's mom didn't chastise him for calling people names. Hell, she might have been the one to give him the idea. Later on that day someone threw a beer can at us from a pickup truck. We weren't holding hands, though, so it's possible that it was just some random asshole. There were a lot of them around. It didn't matter whether or not you were gay—just having tits was reason enough to get harassed.

Seattle would be a much better place to spend summer vacation. And this was Pride weekend, too! If only we could be on Capitol Hill, holding hands, topless except for a few strips of strategically-placed duct tape. Surrounded by Family instead of, well, family. I sighed and flipped a page of *Beebo Brinker*. After a few paragraphs I realized that I hadn't been paying attention for a good half-chapter. No idea what was going on with the plot. I tossed it onto the couch. "If only Lisa were here," I thought, and slipped my hand down the front of my jeans. I wasn't particularly horny, just bored, so instead of trying to get myself off I just played around, idly twirling my wiry pubic hair, stroking my inner lips. My belt was cinched a little too tight, so I unbuckled it and slid my hand down again.

As I fooled around (middle finger circling my hole, sometimes rubbing against my clit) I imagined Lisa and me as twilight lovers, strange bedfellows. We would court in the tangled streets of Greenwich Village, dodge cops, recite passwords to get into secret underground bars. It all seemed terribly romantic. She would be the butch, of course, and I would be the femme. I had a shaved head, but could rock the platform heels like a drag queen, and loved getting dolled up for a night on the town. Lisa had long hair and knew how to accessorize, but had this way of standing, thumbs hooked boyishly into her pockets, square jaw set just so, that made me melt into those arms that were toned by hours of basketball. I smiled a little, picturing her in a man's suit with me on her arm. My fingers started focusing more attention on my clit. I spread my legs a little wider and started circling the hood, sometimes dipping down for a bit of homemade lube. The vibrator I had bought at Babeland during the first week at school was at home, buried under my winter clothes, but I managed to bring myself almost to the edge of orgasm without any problem. I felt myself come closer to coming and started to curl my toes. I gripped the couch cushion hard with my other hand, but before I could really start to let go I heard a knock at the front door.

I froze, then pulled my hand out of my pants. Rolling off the couch I checked my watch. 10:15–who would be coming by this late? The chain was on the door so I opened it a few inches, cautiously, and instantly recognized the strong profile of my girlfriend.

"Lisa!" I gasped, and with no preamble slammed the door in her face. After a minute of fumbling I got the chain unhooked and flung the door open again.

"What are you doing here?" I whispered, pulling her inside. She grinned and kissed me on the lips. She was still in her catering uniform—black dress slacks, white button-down shirt, and a bow tie. Her hair was pulled back in a ponytail, and little diamond studs glittered in her ears. I looked her up and down and felt the itch between my legs grow even more insistent.

"I was at a wedding tonight, right? Only the groom never showed up. We waited for a couple hours, but finally asked if we could leave. Still got paid, so I don't mind."

I laughed. "That's awful! Poor straight woman."

Lisa shrugged. "Means more time with my girl, is all. Told Dad I was going to a movie with my ex-boyfriend. Said I was thinking about getting back together with him. Got so excited he almost wet himself. He warned me to take off the bow tie, but I thought you'd like it if I kept it on."

I grinned sheepishly. "Who knows, maybe your ex has a thing for girls in ties."

"Actually, I know he would. He's gay, too. Figures, the only dyke and the only faggot in the entire high school would end up dating." She looked down and furrowed her brow. "Did I get you out of the bathroom or something?"

I followed her gaze. The ends of my belt were flapping loosely, I must have forgotten to buckle it before answering the door. "Oh! Um, no. I was just, uh . . ."

She eyed me with mock sternness. "Jaclyn Krause, were you masturbating on the job? Right next to where a sweet, innocent little boy lies sleeping? Whatever would Focus on the Family think?"

I shrugged weakly. Teasing always makes me flustered. She knew that, so taking advantage of my momentary speechlessness she took my still-sticky right hand and lifted it to her lips. Kissing it like a courtier she led me back to the couch.

Lips close to my ear she murmured, "Is his door closed?"

"Yes," I gasped, squirming with pleasure from the sensation of her hot breath on my neck. "Oh, yes."

She pushed me down onto the couch. "Ow!" I exclaimed as something hard pressed against my shoulder blade. I reached under and pulled out the book I had been reading earlier. Before I could drop it to the floor Lisa grabbed it.

"*Beebo Brinker*? You were jilling off to this?" An eyebrow cocked skeptically.

"No . . . not exactly," I said. "I was just . . . um, thinking about stuff."

"About what, exactly?" She tossed the book aside and straddled my hips, running her hands over my scalp.

"About . . ." I felt myself start to blush. "About what it was like back then. What it would have been like. Me and you, against the world. You in a tie, me in a dress. Following all those rules that were *so* against the rules."

"I read all of Ann Bannon's stuff when I was first coming out as a dyke. Took them from the shelf of the Barnes and Noble, but stood in the Religion section to read them. You know the one problem with those books?" she asked, slipping her hand up my shirt. One finger just snuck under my bra, stroking the curve of my breast. "They tell you to get to the city, the Village. How to meet the femme—or butch—of your dreams. But you know the parts they leave out?" With sudden, swift, practiced movements she got my shirt up and over my head, unhooked my bra, and draped them on top of the book. She dipped her head to take one of my nipples into her mouth, worrying it gently with her teeth, tweaking the other one with her hand. I started to pant, and moved my pubic bone against her, wordlessly begging for more.

"What . . . mmm . . . what do they leave out?"

Lisa lifted her head and looked into my eyes, a mischievous smile showing her little white teeth. "They don't tell you how to actually *do it*. Don't tell how to make another girl come in your hands. Had to figure that part out for myself."

She unbuttoned my jeans. I lifted my hips to help her slide them off, and she chuckled at the sight of my underwear, hot pink boy-cut briefs. They were damp at the crotch. She pulled them down my thighs, and once they were off went back to toying with my nipples, nibbling on my earlobe.

Inside my head was all color and noise, but I tried to stay quiet so Mikey wouldn't wake up. Still, I couldn't help letting out a squeak when her hand, with its long fingers and trimmed nails, started pressing against the mouth of my cunt. I closed my eyes and tilted my head back, knowing she loved the ways that I responded to her touch.

I was so wet that she slipped one finger, and then another, and then a third into me without a pause. As she started to rock them in and out, her thumb began playing around my clit. I sighed heavily, and kissed her hard so that the sounds I was making would go directly from my mouth into hers. I slid my palms down the waistband of her slacks, held on to her ass cheeks with both hands as I tried to press her deeper into me. My eyes opened and locked with hers. She was flushed too, breathing hard, and I thought about what a sight we made. Me, naked, spread open and wanting. Her a picture of decorum in black and white, pinning me down, watching my every move. She let out a low laugh every time I whimpered, moved against her, threw my head back in ecstasy.

She teased me, sometimes making me chase her hand with my cunt, other times filling me so deeply I felt pinned against the couch. When she started stroking the sides of my clit gently but firmly, slowly at first and then speeding up, slowing down, trying to find my rhythm, I pulled away from her mouth and latched on to her neck. I bit and sucked at her skin, the slightly sour tang of her sweat on my tongue, careful not to leave semicircles of teeth anywhere that couldn't be covered by a T-shirt. Moans were deep in my belly and chest, and a few escaped. She whispered into my ear, asking me how it felt, how I liked having her inside me, just how far I was willing to go with her.

Finally I just had to come. As I pumped myself onto her hand I felt like I was about to explode, eyes screwed tight, jaw clenched, lights flashing, and a silent scream building in my throat. After what seemed like forever I fell back onto the couch, sticky with sweat, and looked up into Lisa's face hovering over me. She was still grinning, eyes sparkling with delight. I listened carefully and heard nothing from the other room, thank heaven.

"So, not the worst babysitting gig in the world, right?"

I purred contentedly. "Much better than doing math homework." She moved off me. I lunged forward and made a playful swipe at her belt, but she scooted further down on the couch and swatted my hand away.

"What time are his parents getting home?"

"In . . ." I glanced at the clock. "Shit! Five minutes. You'd better go. I wish there was time to fool around more. Get you out of those pants, show you how much *I* like a girl in a tie."

"Another time, babe. Besides, weren't all those butches stone?"

"Think so. But you're not!"

"Damn right. You've got too pretty a mouth for that, sweet thing."

I flushed and started putting my clothes back on. "You drove here?"

She nodded.

"Go wait in the car. I'll be out soon." I kissed her on the cheek and she ducked out the back door. Just in time. Mikey's parents pulled up in the driveway just as the door was closing behind her. I saw her dart past the front windows as they came in through the front.

I made small talk with the parents and collected my thirty-five dollars. I had told them I shaved my head because I had been cast as a cancer patient in a school play right before the end of the year. I didn't like babysitting much, but didn't want to get blackballed in the neighborhood. Luckily I could count on my parents not to spread the word.

Before finding Lisa's car, I stopped on the well-lit porch, pulled out my compact and some lipstick, and made sure my lips were a perfect cherry red. I may not be a textbook femme, but there's nothing like leaving another girl's breasts, belly, and cunt stained with your mouth. Capping the tube I ran down the street, grateful for the cover of night, grateful that girls like me no longer needed it to survive.

EARTHY

ANNA WATSON

I LIKED TO MAKE HER get sweaty. I liked the way she smelled—a juicy cross between celery and grapefruit rind, and I liked the way she tasted. In the summer heat, her body stuck delectably to mine when we fucked, her face turned rosy, and drops of sweat broke out along her hairline and on her upper lip, all ready to be lapped up with my tongue. She complained that on humid days the inside of her thighs stuck together, and I liked to think about that, sometimes even pass a hand up under her skirt when we were alone, just to feel it. Moist, hot, salty. She was sexy sweaty.

It wasn't something she was all that comfortable with, actually. Some of her earliest memories were of being in the bathroom in the morning, watching her mom use a lot of sprays as she got dressed: Aqua Net, Right Guard, something she spritzed in her shoes, perfume. The whole bathroom would fog up with sweet, sharp smells. Christine still used some of those sprays—her guilty little secret. So at the beginning of the weekend when I said, "No sprays," she groaned. We were going up to my family's cottage in the U.P. now that summer classes were over, and all I could think about was getting her naked and sweaty. I just couldn't wait to get that first funky whiff, and I grinned big at her as she rolled her eyes and shook her head. She said she hated it, but I knew she would do it for me. My quirky seventh-grade health teacher once said, "Americans are in and out of soapy water way more than is good for them." Amen!

It was a regular Michigan summer, vibrating with humidity and heat. We cranked the air conditioning in the car, but by the time we'd been on the road about an hour, I was starting to smell her. She heard me sniffing and wrinkled her own cute little nose, going, "God, Alana, you're such a freak! I would never ask you to do this for me!"

The truth is I sweat very little, and you can barely smell it when I do, something Christine says she would kill for. She herself sweats like nobody's business, as she says, and like a healthy, desirable, totally yummy girl, according to yours truly.

We stopped for lunch at our favorite diner in a small town near the lake. I could tell Christine felt a little self-conscious, but it was pure bliss sitting next to her on the slick vinyl of the booth, feeding her little bites of my grilled cheese sandwich, feeling her lick the grease off my fingers. Just to get close enough to breathe deep and thank the good lord.

It was slightly cooler up at the lake, with the hint of a breeze. Now that we were on our own again, Christine started to relax, singing to herself as she looked out the window. We pulled up to the cottage and I jumped out, throwing back my head and sniffing like a dog the way I always do, gathering up the precious smells of lake water, dried grass, my mom's scraggly roses—smells that relaxed and welcomed me the way they had every summer of my whole life. Christine got out more slowly, stretching and yawning. Her blouse was sticking to her back and I saw her discreetly tugging her skirt to get it out of her butt crack. I like thinking about the way bodies interact with clothes, how they feel, how they smell, but Christine hates it when I notice her adjusting herself, and she frowned at me. I just smiled, imagining how, when I got her naked later, I would nuzzle the damp, red indentation that this particular skirt made on her soft white belly.

"You're making me hard," I murmured, and she couldn't stop herself from giggling.

"Promises, promises!" she said, then made a break for the water. I dropped the bag of food I was carrying and ran after her. One of the nicest things about the cottage was that we had a tiny, tiny little cove on the lake, secluded and private, and even though there were neighbors not too far away, no one could see onto our little bit of a beach unless they were going by in a boat. I grabbed Christine before she reached the water—no way was she going to rinse off that sweat she'd been building up in the car. I lowered her to the ground and pinned her arms above her head, rubbing my face all over the damp fabric of her shirt, taking deep sniffs. She wriggled and complained, but she was laughing, too.

"Baby, you know I think you smell fantastic," I said, my eyes closed. I felt like I was sampling the finest wine, letting it slip over the palate of my nose, teasing out the hidden secrets of its essence. I got fully on top of her, and she welcomed me, relaxing, melting under me, allowing her pussy to rise up. I was packing, and she made that little sound of pleasure that about killed me—the one she always made when she got up close and personal with my dick—a pleased and lascivious whimper. I kept still as she humped up, knowing how much she liked to know it was safe for her to go crazy because I was in control. I kissed her sweaty neck, taking long swipes with my tongue. I knew there was sweat pooling in her bra, under her fabulous tits, and I lifted her blouse to take a tongueful. She squirmed beneath me, panting, hugging me to her. This was the part I loved, when she forgot she was a decorous femme, concerned with appearance and body odor, and became a wanton slut, offering up her lush body with all its earthy delights. I slipped my hands under her skirt to tease the sweaty crack of her ass, and we lay there, kissing softly, then harder, letting the heat rise up around us.

"Alana, do me, baby," she moaned into my neck, and my dick jumped with pleasure. I rolled off her and tore off her clothes. I breathed deep as she got up on her hands and knees and swished her chunky ass back and forth, tempting me. I licked a trail down her back—sweaty—under her arms, across the back of her neck. She shuddered and gasped, saying my name. I stepped back for a moment to admire the view. I could see her ass cheeks quivering as she moved for me. I could see her swollen clit poking out through the damp curls of her twat. I adored how hairy she was down there, her abundant bush. I took her around the waist and pulled her close.

We were deep into the nasty, me humping her from behind, her huffing and juddering as I pounded her, when we heard a loud

"Hilooo!"—a neighborly trill. We fell all over ourselves trying to get decent. At the last moment Christine shoved her hopelessly tangled clothing under a big piece of driftwood and splashed naked into the water. It was a little easier for me, since I hadn't taken off any clothes, and I was straightening my shirt when Mrs. Saarinen came tripping down to the beach.

There are two kinds of folks who live at the lake (well, three if you count the tourists): people who have seasonal cottages—little more than shacks, really, but right on the lake—and people who have big, year-round sprawling estates, like Mrs. Saarinen. She was our closest neighbor, and I used to babysit her boys when I was in high school, enjoying the chance to get away from the crowded cottage where my family jostled and joshed each other. I loved spending time in the Saarinens' pristine, air-conditioned house, snooping around after the boys were asleep, eating everything in the kitchen, and watching tons of TV. It didn't hurt that I'd always had a crush on Mrs. Saarinen, with her blonde bob and perky little boobies.

"I heard your car drive up!" she announced cheerfully, flipping back a shining lock of hair. She was dressed for tennis and looked hearty and fit. The fact that Christine and I had just been fucking combined with how attractive I'd always found Mrs. Saarinen was giving me trouble and I couldn't think of anything to say. Christine waved jauntily from the water and began swimming to and fro. I had to stifle a laugh as I got a flash of her ass, breaching the water like a sea creature.

"I brought you some snickerdoodles!" Mrs. Saarinen sang out, thrusting a large Tupperware container into my hands. I hoped she couldn't smell Christine's pussy on my fingers; I sure could. I grinned at her, sure I was blushing. She grinned back, and for a moment I got the idea that she knew exactly what we'd been doing and that she was getting a little thrill from having interrupted us.

We settled in for a neighborly chat, discussing the temperature of the water, the quality of this summer's tourists and their lack of sense with jet skis. She told me she was alone for the week, with both boys at summer camp and her husband on a business trip. After a while, she sashayed off to her tennis lesson. Christine came splashing out of the water, saying she felt like a prune and that she'd thought I was never going to stop flirting with that woman, and then she sashayed off, too, leaving me to unload the car. I had hoped we were going to finish what we'd started earlier. But all in good time, if I knew my baby, so I grabbed a couple of snickerdoodles—chewy and amazing—and popped the trunk.

When I'd finished unloading, I was as sweaty as I ever get. Christine, bless her, had stuck a couple of beers in the cooler, and I cracked one open as I sat at the kitchen table listening to her putter around in the bedroom. She came out naked to get her own beer, absentmindedly smoothing her skin with the sweating bottle, torturing me, and having a good time doing it.

"Baby," I said, but she interrupted.

"What do you know about that Mrs. Saarinen?" she asked.

"Huh?" Mrs. Saarinen was definitely not who I'd been thinking about.

"I mean, do you get the feeling she thinks we're interesting?"

I took a drink of my beer and we exchanged knowing looks. "You mean you think she's one of those kinds of straight women?" I asked. She nodded, looking smug.

"A femme's nightmare," Christine called them, the straight women who flirted with me so blatantly you would swear they were queer. The first time it happened was freshman year, when Christine and I were out on a date. The waitress at the restaurant hovered over me, coming back to check on me, refilling my water glass a hundred times so she could bend over and show me her cleavage and ignoring Christine's repeated requests to see the dessert tray. When we were walking back to campus Christine said, "What do you think she would have done if you'd called her on that? I mean, if you'd grabbed her tit or something?" She'd been grumpy about it for the rest of the evening, even though she'd tried to hide it.

These days we were rock solid as a couple, but she still hated it when straight women came on to me like that. Personally, I thought it was kind of cute—I mean, they can't really help themselves, the poor dears. It's the seductive power of the butch, don't you know.

"I think we should go spy on her."

"Mrs. Saarinen? What the fuck for?" But the idea was interesting, and I could feel a flicker of my teenage crush coming even more alive. And big love for my baby, who was such a bunch of fun.

Instead of answering me, she set down her bottle of beer. "It's so hot!" she moaned, heading for my parents' bedroom, where there was a shower in the bathroom. I followed her expectantly. I know it's a little juvenile, but it always gave me a special thrill to fuck Christine on my parents' bed. Who knew? I might even have been conceived on that bed.

"Come on, bad boy," said Christine, adjusting the water, then stepping in. She wagged a bar of soap at me suggestively, but I didn't need any coaxing. I got naked and got in beside her, but instead of reaching out for me with the bubbles, she started to rub the soap over her own tits and belly, getting good and lathered up.

"Turn around."

I turned my back to her, bracing myself against the Plexiglas. She pressed her slippery body against me, shimmying up to my shoulders and down to my ass, the feel of her breasts soft and warm and so fucking hot. She shifted so she could get her arm between us, sliding it up and down in the suds, its width spreading my butt cheeks. I moaned as she cupped my package and slid in some fingers.

"Right where I want you," she murmured in my ear. She held me tight with her other arm, fingers scampering all over my chest. She's a biter and she started really going after my neck and shoulder; I found marks there the next day. I came, thrusting into her hand as she gave me a particularly vicious nip, then I slumped to the floor and let the cool water sluice over me. She straddled me briefly, giving me a view of her plump pussy, drops gathering in the hair and sliding down the inside of her thighs, then pranced out of the shower.

"No sprays!" I managed to call after her. My voice was throaty and weak. She threw me a look over her shoulder and left me there, soggy and spent.

By supper, it was as though we'd never showered. The humidity was way up and the heat was intense. The cabin smelled like all the summers of my childhood: heated wooden walls, hints of mold from the old sofa and chairs, dust, lake, and hamburgers cooking. I breathed deeply as I sliced the plump tomatoes we'd picked up at a farmer's stand, then flared my nostrils as Christine passed me on her way to the fridge. She smelled incredible, just pure animal. I growled and she frowned, muttering, "Dog," but

I could tell she was still sexed up from earlier, and wasn't really mad.

Sure enough, we got to giggling and fooling around while we were doing the dishes. We had our shirts off and I could almost see the wisp of scent leading to my baby's pussy. I kept imagining myself as the hungry hobo in a comic strip, following his nose to where a careless housewife had left an apple pie out on the windowsill to cool.

It was getting dark now, with fireflies starting to come out. We were both enjoying the tension that had been building between us. Christine looked a little sneaky, and I wondered what she had up her sleeve, but was content not to push her. I'd totally forgotten what she'd said about Mrs. Saarinen earlier; all I could think about was how bad I wanted to get into her pants. I'd brought a cigar with me—we both liked a little toke or two now and again—and we sat on the stoop to smoke it, turning our faces into the slight breeze off the lake. Our shirts were still off, but the smoke kept away the worst of the mosquitoes. Fireflies blinked in the dark. Feeling drowsy and lovey, I figured we'd be going in soon for a languid bit of fucking in my parents' bed, but Christine had other ideas.

"I think it's dark enough now," she said, letting out a stream of smoke. "Oh, don't look at me like that! I told you, I want to go spy on that woman."

On Mrs. Saarinen. Right.

"You used to babysit for her, didn't you?"

I was still trying to figure out if she was serious. I don't know why I was wasting my time—of course she was serious.

"Come on, finish this thing. Let's go." She handed me the cigar stub and stretched, her dark hair falling down her back, her bosom like an offering to the star gods. I sucked in one last toke and tried to get my arms around her, but she slipped out of my grasp.

"Come on!"

The Saarinens lived the equivalent of maybe two blocks away, but there weren't any sidewalks or anything. Just a gravel road—no streetlamps. The sky was a blaze of stars, and we were pretty visible, had anyone been around to look. By the time we got to the end of the drive, we had a hopeless case of the giggles. "Shh!" we kept telling each other. "Shh!" I wasn't sure why we were going to spy on Mrs. Saarinen, but at that point, I would have followed my fragrant sweetie just about anywhere.

The Saarinens had a box hedge around their property, and we crouched down behind it, surveying the house. Most of it was dark, except for the kitchen and a room right next to it: the family room, I remembered. I had spent a lot of time in there, watching cable in cool comfort, polishing off boxes of cookies and cartons of ice cream with chocolate sauce. The house was the last one on this little peninsula, and I suppose Mrs. Saarinen had never really had a reason to close the curtains, because, after all, who could be out there? Or maybe she liked the idea that she could get caught. Maybe she was even hoping we would come by—who knows? At any rate, she was there in the family room, plainly visible in the dim light from a table lamp. She was splayed back in a leather recliner, her little tennis skirt rucked up around her belly. Peeping around the shrubbery, we had an amazing view of her as she turned on one of those deluxe vibrators and held it out at arm's length, like she was admiring it.

"Exhibit A," whispered Christine, and we giggled some more. It was a good thing the windows were closed to keep in the AC or she would have heard us for sure. I was pretty much past caring what happened, though. The beers we had been drinking had gone to my head, and it didn't seem all that strange that we were here watching this hot older woman get ready to masturbate. The moist summer air at the lake seemed permeated with fuck energy —I'd been in a state of turn-on for hours, and it was only natural that the other denizens of this sexed-up place would also be panting for relief.

"Come on." Christine tugged at my hand, trying to get me out from behind the greenery. "There's no way she can see us." We sneaked out onto the strip of lawn below the window, staying low. I settled into a sitting position, my legs spread wide, Christine leaning back against me. Her bare back stuck to my chest, and my hands went to her breasts of their own volition just as Mrs. Saarinen brought the vibrator down to her pussy. She and Christine jerked at the same time, a sexy body hiccup. I twisted Christine's nipples and she pressed into me so hard I almost lost my balance and tipped over. Mrs. Saarinen's mouth opened wide in pleasure as she rubbed her pussy all over the fat head of the vibrator, which she kept very still in one hand.

"Oh, god," moaned Christine as I cranked on her nipples. My girl likes some hearty nipple stim. Still, I knew her pussy needed attention, too—god knows, mine did—so I lowered one hand, trailing it over her belly, and danced my fingers past the elastic of her skirt waistband, down to where I discovered she didn't have any panties on at all. We mmmm'd in tandem, and I kept my fingers dancing through all her tangled curls, slick with sweat and juice. Christine adjusted herself, lifting her cunt up to me as I stroked and slid all over her needy pussy. Mrs. Saarinen had wedged the vibrator between her thighs and was using both hands to caress her tits, palming them, rubbing them all around, then grabbing the nipples and yanking, all the time humping the vibrator, all the time with her mouth open in that hungry, silent scream. I got two fingers inside Christine, my thumb on her clit, and she rode me, hands pressed into the dew-damp grass, until I knew just one more thrust would make her come. I pulled out and held her trapped against me while she thrashed her head from side to side and tried to drag my hands back, tried to touch herself. I wouldn't let her, whispering hot in her ear to "Wait, baby, wait," and we watched, breathing hard, until it was clear Mrs. Saarinen was almost there. Then all I had to do was cup my baby's crotch and let her fuck down, once, and she came, and I came, just from rubbing up against Christine's fine, soft ass, and Mrs. Saarinen came, with a piercing squeal we could hear even through the double-plated glass. Christine slumped against me and we tumbled into a limp pile on the grass, kissing all sloppy and loving, humping against each other to milk out the last of that delicious come. I even cried a little, like I do when the love gets to be a little too much for me. Christine licked away my tears and we stayed in each other's arms I don't know how long. When we finally untangled and helped each other to our feet, Mrs. Saarinen was gone and the family room window was dark.

"Do you think she saw us?" Christine asked, for the first time sounding just the tiny bit concerned. I held her hand as we navigated the unlit path back to the cottage, not interested in anything but the fact that I was the luckiest guy in the world, going home to sleep with this wonderful, smart, sexy, good-smelling girl.

In the morning, Christine got up early and made us coffee. It was already hot, sun shining in the window, no breeze to speak of.

The fan we'd turned on during the night made labored noises as it blew heated air around.

"Oh, Alana, please?" Christine said, ducking her head under her arm and taking a whiff, making a sour face.

"No," I said dreamily, my nose in the air. I knew she was dying for a shower, but the smells that had been cooking in the bedroom all night were practically ripe enough for me to eat for breakfast, and I didn't want anything to change. "Oh, honestly!" said Christine huffily, settling back beside me with her coffee. I put mine on the floor and ducked under the sheet to kiss her belly, the unmitigated gnarly fug making me so happy that I groaned out, "Thank you, baby, thank you for not washing," and she relaxed, laughing a little, reaching down to stroke my face. Giving me everything.

THE EVOLUTION OF PARTY GIRL

CHARLOTTE DARE

THE TEMPERATURE IN L.A. had broken eighty by nine a.m., a perfect day for digging my toes in the sand with a Jackie Collins novel at Santa Monica beach. Instead, I was holed up in the stockroom of the Greater Los Angeles Food Bank, sorting donated items into bags and boxes with Erin, a sun-drenched blonde right off a Southern California travel brochure. Certainly not the worst of alternatives.

I smiled to myself as she gathered food items for bagging, her brow wrinkled with intensity as she mixed and matched the best combination. During our Sunday mornings together over the last six weeks, I had become a master of stealing glances, turning away just before she felt the weight of my stare. I'd never been caught, either, until a fantasy of her in a pair of tight volleyball shorts plowing through the sand on a serve return knocked me off my guard.

"Am I the only one working here?" she asked. "What are you staring at?"

I quickly grabbed a jar of gravy and bagged it. "Nothing, it's just funny seeing you taking this so seriously."

"What's that supposed to mean?" The perceived insult turned her tanned cheeks rosy.

"Oh, no offense," I said. "It's just that humanitarianism seemed a foreign concept to you when you first got here."

She threw her hand on her hip and scrunched her face into a sexy scowl. "What would ever give you that impression?"

"You don't remember? You spent the whole first day bitching about how horrible and grimy this place was."

"Cut me some slack, huh? You can't expect anyone to show up the first day of court-ordered community service and be all jazzed about it."

"True," I said. "But, lucky you, it's finally up next Sunday." I tried to sound happy for her, but I was already anticipating the desperate ache of missing her. Despite her effort, I was convinced Erin's philanthropy would last only as long as the judge's sentence.

"Oh, yeah." She pumped her fist and broke into an impromptu dance. "After three long months, I'll be free at last and able to drive again." After calming down, she squared off a cloth bag with two boxes of penne pasta and jarred sauces. "I don't know how anyone can eat this stuff," she said with a sneer.

"Try not eating at all for a day or two or three, and this stuff, as you so snobbishly put it, will taste like it came from Spago."

She sighed, duly chastised. "You're right, Renee. I guess you can take the girl out of the Hills but you can't take the Hills out of the girl."

I playfully nudged her shoulder. "Don't worry. I still say there's hope for you."

She grinned and nudged back. "Maybe I should sell my Mercedes SUV for something smaller, like a Beamer coupe convertible. That'll help the environment, right?"

"Sure. So will your dad grounding his private jet."

"I'll mention that next time I see him, whenever that may be," she said wistfully.

"Busy guy, huh?" I said, but absentee fathers were as unfamiliar to me as trust funds and the taste of Beluga caviar.

"Sometimes I think they bought me that beach house just to get me out of their hair."

"Why would they do that?"

She hesitated for a moment and then pushed her bag aside, resting her elbows on the counter. "I was a wild child," she confessed. "Swiped Mom's Percodan and Valium, got caught in a hot tub with a director's wife on my eighteenth birthday, and got kicked out of prep school for ditching class. Forget an Ivy League school after that. I don't need to tell you how my Harvard-educated father felt about his only child graduating State college. And then the DUI. I guess I can't blame them for sending their lawyer to bail me out."

"That's a hard lesson," I offered.

"I mean, what do they expect when they give a kid everything and don't show her what to do with it all?" Her brooding eyes told me she revealed more than she wanted to, but it was too late to take it back. She was human and understood anguish. Suddenly, my attraction to her wasn't so superficial. It was okay to love her, or whatever I felt for her that had me in this grip. "So." Her voice spiked with that it's-time-to-change-the-subject urgency. "You really volunteered for this?"

I nodded. "Doesn't anyone in this town do good without being ordered to by the court?"

"Sure they do," she said. "On the advice of their tax attorney," she added with a wink.

"To be honest, this wasn't exactly my idea," I said. "I didn't know anyone when I transferred from the Connecticut office. My dad said volunteering was a great way to meet people, and he was right. I met you, didn't I?"

Erin smiled, and as she stretched her lean body across the counter for another bag, I inhaled an enticing blend of freshly laundered clothes and something floral by Ralph Lauren.

"It was a lucky thing for me, too," she said. "I would've gone insane if you hadn't been here."

For a moment, I imagined she was flirting. "So I guess you'll be glad never to see the inside of this joint again."

She gave a noncommittal shrug as she looked for a jar of peanut butter to pair with a box of crackers.

I glanced at her, hoping the comment would've elicited some clue as to where we stood now that her hellish nightmare of self-sacrifice was almost over. "Think we'll still be friends after next week?" I braced myself for another shrug.

"What do you think?" she challenged.

"Oh, of course we will," I drawled. "You're only the daughter of a rich Hollywood producer who hits a different A-list party every night of the week. While I, on the other hand, adjust car insurance claims and bowl. We're obviously meant to be BFFs."

She giggled. "That's such an exaggeration. I only do an A-list party twice a week."

I laughed, but the real possibility of never seeing Erin again ripped the usual airiness from my disposition.

"I tell you what. To prove I'm sincere, I want you to come out to the Palms with my friends and me Saturday night. They're a lot of fun. I think you'll have a great time."

"What's the Palms?"

"The lesbian bar on Santa Monica." She eyed me curiously. "You're a lesbian and you don't know what the Palms is?"

"I've only lived here for two months."

"Then Saturday night's going to be your coming-out party."

◆

CRAMMED ELBOW-TO-ELBOW around a small table with Erin and her harem of three, I studied the bevy of babes undulating on the packed dance floor. They were all attractive in unique and interesting ways, but nobody captured my attention the way Erin did whenever she was anywhere in the vicinity.

She leaned into me and shouted into my ear, "Is this place awesome or what?"

Being in a noisy bar with a hot woman definitely had its perks. I shivered as her lips ever so slightly grazed my ear, and then shouted back, "I feel like Captain Kirk in that *Star Trek* episode where the Enterprise lands on a planet full of beautiful women. Except on this planet, they're all lesbians."

Erin laughed. "I'm becoming an astronaut if they discover that planet really exists. So, are you having a good time?"

I nodded, but in truth, I felt like I was on another planet. I had about five years on Erin and her friends, and while I was ready to call it a night, maybe get a cup of coffee alone with Erin, these gals showed no signs of winding down.

"Isn't it time for another round?" asked Jordan, a famous actress's bisexual daughter.

Knowing I had already depleted my entertainment slush fund for the week, I shook my head and played it off. "Not me. I'm watching my calories."

Erin's eyes darted between me and her friends. "Me, too. I feel like the before photo in a Jenny Craig ad."

Jordan rolled her eyes at the other two girls and signaled them to follow her to the bar.

Erin's creamy skin glistened with a light mist of sweat from leading her crew in the Cupid Shuffle earlier. "When are you going to ask me to dance?" she asked, blotting her forehead with a cocktail napkin.

I looked at my watch. "Wait a minute . . ." A long pause for dramatic effect. "Okay, now."

She pulled me up by my wrist and weaved through the crowd, towing me along until we reached the center of the dance floor.

"I know you're into alternative rock, but you've got some hot moves," she said, swaying closer to me.

A dancer I was not, but once we locked thighs and started bumping and grinding to the driving house music, dance skills were of little relevance.

She placed my hands on her hips and gyrated wildly, throwing her arms into the air, bellowing out an "*ooit-ooit*" every now and then when the mood struck her. Whipping her hair around like a stripper, she was sexy and uninhibited, and aroused in me a level of desire I'd never experienced before.

"You're really wild, you know that," I said with a fascinated smile.

She grinned back and kissed me—a hot, wet kiss that surged all the way down to my pussy.

"Have you ever driven a woman crazy?" I asked as she fondled the ends of my hair. "I mean literally out of her mind?"

"Not yet," she said, pecking at my lips, "but you like volunteering for things."

After a moment of intense tongue play we were joined by the girlfriends, who crowded us on the dance floor, air humping both of us from behind. Josie, the exotic daughter of a Kuwaiti oil tycoon, handed Erin an appletini, which she guzzled like water.

"I hope we're not interrupting anything," Josie slurred, shaking her ass against Erin's.

Before I realized it was Jordan's unsteady Absolut Royal Fuck splashing on my sandals, they had swarmed Erin and squeezed me out.

"I was just going to hit the ladies' room," I shouted and left her to cavort with her friends.

At last call, the girls returned to our table, where I sat contriving a smile.

"Where'd you go? I thought you were coming back out to dance," Erin said.

I shook my head and thought I caught Claire drilling me with a contemptuous glare. "Us older gals can't shake it all night long like you girls can."

Erin scoffed. "*Older gals*. Like twenty-nine is so old. You think you can drag yourself to the diner with us? I'm dying for a goat cheese omelet."

"No, thanks. I better head home. I have to get up early tomorrow."

Erin surprised me with a look of genuine disappointment. "Oh, okay . . . Are you sure?"

"Come on, Erin. Let's beat it," Claire said, with another glare in my direction.

"I'll see you bright and early tomorrow," I reminded her as the girls jostled her away from me through the crowd.

As Erin's blonde hair submerged into the sea of blondes exiting, a wave of longing and nausea swept over me. What was I doing sabotaging the greatest thing that happened to me in ages? Meeting Erin sparked renewed hope. Single for most of my twenties, I had begun to believe a woman I could connect with simply didn't exist. I'd met women who were attractive, intelligent, socially aware, and fun to be with, but scoring all of those qualities in one person seemed impossible, until Erin. Okay, maybe I was being too generous in the "socially aware" department, but for a face like hers, who wouldn't?

◆

THE NEXT MORNING I AWOKE still queasy for a variety of reasons, not the least of which was the fact that once Erin completed her court-ordered community service, more than likely our delicate friendship would burn off like morning smog over Malibu. That's just how these things worked out.

Erin yawned for the fourth time as she absently arranged canned goods in a box.

"You're awfully quiet," I said.

She stopped, looked in my eyes, and shrugged.

I glanced away for a moment, overcome by the power of her lightning blues and those irresistible lips dabbed with tangerine gloss. "What's the matter? Don't tell me you're going to miss this place after today?"

"It's not the place I'm going to miss," she said coldly.

"What do you mean?"

She frowned. "I thought things were going pretty decent with us. For a while last night, I thought we were finally turning the corner. But you pretty much showed me that's not gonna happen."

"Erin, I like you a lot, but we move in such different circles."

"And that's a problem?"

"We're so opposite. I'm from a small town back East, and this L.A. lifestyle can be overwhelming, to say the least. I'm not a big partier. I never have been."

"Who said you have to be? If we like each other, why can't we just be together?"

"I want to be with someone I can settle down with eventually."

She shot me an indignant glare. "So my suspicions were right. You do think all I wanna do is party."

"You're young and a member of the Hollywood Super-clique. Why shouldn't you?"

"That's not all I'm about, Renee. I'm not the shallow, self-absorbed party girl you think I am. You're stereotyping me, and it isn't fair." She stormed out of the storeroom in a pout.

I chased after her but stopped short of trailing her into the bathroom. Brilliant, Renee. Instead of just telling her I was in love with her, I insulted her and made her cry.

After about fifteen minutes, she returned to her post at the counter, making sure she was at the end as far away from me as possible.

"Erin, I'm sorry," I said in a soft voice.

She didn't look up.

"Erin, I said I was sorry."

"I heard you."

I slid my box of nonperishables down toward her. "I'm sorry I stereotyped you. It was very uncool of me." I waited a moment to see if she'd soften. "But in all honesty, aside from our philosophical Sunday morning chats about life, I haven't seen any other side of you."

"You haven't given me the chance to show you. Have you ever asked me to dinner at that Thai-fusion place you rave about? No. Or to your favorite bookstore? Or the beach, even though I always say how much I love playing volleyball? No, you haven't. But when I ask you to hang out with my friends because I can't figure out what you really think of me, you use the occasion to slam me."

She resumed packing the box to the point nobody would be able to move it without a forklift. I stole her hands away from the cans and offered a repentant smile. "Erin, do you want to know what I really think of you?"

She shrugged with a heavy sigh.

"I think you're incredible," I gushed.

She smiled tentatively, so sweet, so vulnerable I wanted to scoop her up in my arms and take her home. Suddenly, she pulled me toward her and kissed me, gliding her fruity lips over mine.

I slipped my arms around her neck and tingled when she pressed her soft body against me. As our tongues intimately reacquainted themselves, my fingers explored her supple face and the curve of her neck, flitting down over the blonde fuzz on her upper back.

"I want you, Renee," she breathed. Her hands crept up the back of my shirt, flicked open my bra, and began eagerly massaging my breasts. Her thumbs grazed across my hard nipples, shooting a jolt of excitement through me.

"Here?" I asked, but I'd already fallen into the ecstasy of her touch.

"Yeah, right here, right now." She tugged at the waistband of my checkered Bermudas.

"But it's almost eleven," I protested, trying to contain her legion of roaming hands. "Luis will be here any minute."

"He never gets here before noon on Sundays," she reminded me.

"But someone might . . ."

"Shut up and fuck me, Renee," she demanded. She dropped her satiny running shorts to her ankles and ripped down my zipper.

"No tan line," I remarked with delight and lowered her thong, revealing a sexy, bronzed hardwood floor.

She thrust herself into my thigh as I squeezed her caramel buns, nearly lifting her off the floor. I tickled behind her ear with my tongue, and she groaned, streaming hot breath against the side of my face. I couldn't believe how badly I craved her, every inch of her, from those golden coconut-scented shoulders to her dainty pink toes.

She pulled up my shirt along with hers and rubbed her stomach and breasts against mine as she moaned into my ear. She twisted my nipples, delivering a warm, glorious ache to my clit.

I couldn't stand it anymore. I grabbed her hand and shoved it between my legs. She needed no further directing as all four fingers began exploring me.

She groaned loudly when I slid inside of her. We held each other tightly as both our fingers pumped in and out of each other, slowly at first until we found our natural rhythm. We fucked each other harder and faster as our cries of pleasure escalated.

Her bobbing palomino ponytail tickled my hand, which was supporting her wild backward lurches. "Mmm, Renee, this feels so good," she gasped.

Heavy breathing and whimpers of pleasure enveloped the cramped stockroom.

"Faster, Renee, faster, I'm coming," she whispered in my ear.

"Me too, baby."

"Fuck me harder," she cried and feverishly pumped her pelvis into my hand.

Every muscle in my body tensed. I clutched Erin with all my strength, as we brought each other to resounding climax.

Beaded with perspiration, we collapsed together against the counter behind us. After we tasted each other on our fingers, we kissed, glowing with satisfaction.

"I never knew breaking the law could reap such awesome rewards." Erin laughed. She wrapped her arms around my waist and wiggled me playfully.

I rolled my eyes. "You get another DUI and you'll be doing this in a prison shower . . . whether you want to or not."

"I'm just kidding. My days of reckless irresponsibility are over. You wouldn't put up with it for five minutes, would you?"

"Not even three," I insisted and kissed the tiny beauty mark on her chin. "So now what?"

"Same time next week?"

"Oh, is that how it is? You stroll in from your ritzy Malibu beach house and molest me while I'm trying to help those less fortunate?"

"What do you mean, *you*?" she asked, feigning offense. "You think you're the only do-gooder around here willing to give up a Sunday morning?"

I smiled. "I'm sorry. I shouldn't have assumed."

She nodded graciously as she packed up her last box.

"So, then, I'll meet you here next week?" I asked.

"No, we'll ride in together, from my ritzy Malibu beach house after we crawl out of my ritzy Egyptian cotton sheets. Is that all right with you?"

I grabbed her arms, yanked her toward me, and gave her a long, sensual kiss. "I'm glad you're still up for volunteering."

"I think I can get into this humanitarianism thingy—especially if this is how we'll spend our breaks." She raised her eyebrows lustfully and licked my cheek.

This must be what they mean by the joy of giving.

HOLY FUCK

GENEVA KING

SISTER WIVES

I TOWED THEIR CAR after it broke down on a deserted stretch of the highway. The three of us squeezed into my truck and made small talk on the way back to town. Sister wives, they told me. When I asked about the recent compound arrests, they looked at me disdainfully and told me they weren't that kind of Mormon.

I called them Wife 1 and Wife 2, like characters in a Dr. Seuss book. The younger one sat in the middle, her body pressed against my side. She had the friendly smile, but it was the other one who caught my attention, the one with the tight bun and disapproving frown, as if she knew exactly what I was thinking about every time I looked in her direction. For some reason, I always pick the difficult one.

I took their car to the mechanic. Their husband couldn't get them until the next day and they were too far to call a friend, so I offered them the room in my apartment for the night. Wife 1 hesitated, but Wife 2 agreed willingly, the same way she went into my arms later that night, her lips pressing into mine with the timidity of someone who isn't really experienced but eager to explore and get explored.

Wife 1 walked in on us and turned to flee, a red flush spreading over her cheeks, but Wife 2 simply held out her hand as if she hadn't been caught rubbing her cunt over my thigh that was now streaked with her juices while I sucked her nipples.

I remained silent for fear of scaring her off. Lust fought with good sense, but finally she stepped towards us and allowed Wife 2 to kiss her palm. Wife 2 and I turned our attention to her, undressing her, letting down her beautiful hair, fondling her body, until she was as horny as we were and God himself couldn't have stopped her.

I kissed a trail down her soft skin until I reached her full thighs, guessing what she needed wasn't the fullness of a cock. I drew my tongue over her engorged clit; she bucked in surprise, grabbing at my hair and I knew I had made the right choice. Wife 2 coached her, kissing her, distracting her so she could relax enough to enjoy what I was giving her.

In the morning, the bun was back, but the eyes were softer. The husband offered to pay me for my help, but I refused, telling him I was happy to have kept his wives safe.

P.K.

SHE WAS A P.K. (Preacher's Kid) and took great pleasure in living up to the stereotype. Between that and her role as the youngest of six, she had some serious issues that I was happy to let her work out on me.

She held every set of eyes with her too-short skirt and tight top. She knew how to walk, talk, and flirt so the guys at the bar fell over themselves buying her drinks, hoping to score a night with her. After she'd had her fill, she led me out of the crowded club to the narrow alley beside it. The thud of the music was the only thing covering my overexcited heartbeat.

She smiled innocently, even as she worked her way into my panties.

"Are you even old enough to be drinking?"

She shrugged, never stopping or looking away. "I will be next year. Why? Worried?"

And then she flicked my sweet spot and the only thing I worried about was someone stumbling upon us and interrupting the delicious torture she was inflicting on me.

"You're not used to being fucked." It wasn't a question.

All I could do was whimper pitifully in response. She had me up against the wall, clutching her as she thrust her finger—no, fingers, she'd added another—inside me. This young woman, making my eyes roll back into my head as she whispered all the dirty things she wanted to do to me in that alley, fucking me like she had years of experience under her belt. Maybe she did. She was a P.K.

As I came, I felt like I momentarily left my body. I sagged against the grimy wall, not caring about what might end up on my shirt or exposed skin. She pressed her fingers to my mouth so I could lick them clean. I complied and reached for her. She danced out of my reach, waved those same fingers at me, then disappeared into the crowded parking lot.

PROFESSOR

MY ART HISTORY PROFESSOR had a small dot in the middle of her forehead. A bindi, which she later explained represented a third eye.

She showed me pictures of the deities: Krishna's blue skin, ones with multiple sets of arms, and even an elephant with the same playful smile as the woman sitting across from me.

We locked ourselves in her office. I cleared her desk and tied a scarf securely over her eyes; even the shiny third one so she couldn't see me touching her, couldn't anticipate my moves. I donned my strap-on, imagining I was one of her gods, wishing that I had an extra set of hands to caress her with. The soft skin between her breasts. The full nipples begging to be pinched. The soft expanse of stomach that I now gripped as I pressed my cock against her lips. Gently. Just a little taste.

"More."

I dipped in further, stopping halfway and pulling out. Her mouth was open, her chest rising as her breath came faster.

"More." This time it was less of a request and more of a command. I filled her with the cock until she grunted, raising her hips so I could get deeper. I moved slowly within her, trying to draw it out, even as my own need yelled at me to pay it some attention.

I drew her legs over my shoulders, feeling the tense muscles in her thighs. Her shiny painted toes called for me to kiss them. And so I did, capturing a tiny toe between my teeth. She yelled and clutched her breasts, squeezing her nipples as her orgasm ran through her body.

Looking down at her sprawled on her desk, limbs splayed, hair matted and not caring, I wondered if this was how it felt to be a god. I still hadn't released her trembling legs, and for the first time, got a good look at her slit. Climbing on top of her, I pressed my body against her until my pussy could rub against her thigh and I humped her until we both cried out, her teeth digging into my shoulder.

Before I left, I went down on her. Part of me needed to finally taste her. Another part needed to feel the power of making her come one last time.

ANOTHER'S WOMAN

I FELL IN LUST with my best friend's brother's girlfriend, a modern American woman in all ways except for the bright blue scarf artfully wrapped around her head.

We met at a couple's movie night and chatted long after the others lay snoring on the couch. I touched the smooth silk of her head gear, letting the shiny fabric run through my fingers.

"Beautiful."

We both knew I didn't give a damn about the scarf. She licked her lips, her eyes scanning the other occupants in the room.

With a last look at her sleeping boyfriend, she eased him off her lap and inclined her head towards the stairway.

I expected to be the one to take the lead and initiate her to the pleasures of sapphic lovemaking, but she surprised me by pushing me onto the narrow bed. The first kiss tasted sweet. Glorious. Then she took control, staking her claim on my mouth and face.

She inched down until her head bobbed between my legs, the bright blue contrasting with my brown skin. Her tongue flicked my hole and stroked my clit until I quivered under her.

But she wouldn't give me the release I craved. She sat back, drawing the scarf from around her head, revealing the wavy hair beneath. Before I could move, she'd grabbed my wrists and tied me to the headboard.

I glared at her. She laughed.

"You look upset." Her fingertips grazed my stomach until I squirmed.

She continued as if she didn't notice my distress. "I'm a taken woman, you know. You shouldn't be trying to hit on me."

"But, I—" I tried to stammer my innocence, but she silenced me.

"You can't expect to go unpunished."

There was a wicked gleam in her eye as she went back down. This woman who I had thought was so straitlaced and shy was teasing me with her hot breath, blowing over my lips. She drew her tongue across me so lightly I thought I had imagined it.

"Damn—"

She looked up, icily calm. "If they wake up, I'll have to stop."

That was a sobering thought. I clenched my teeth together as she tormented me. Tears ran down my face, but I didn't say a word, just dug my nails into my palms until she gave me the release I needed.

Afterwards, she lay next to me and we kissed until we feel asleep. I tried to pleasure her, maybe exact a little revenge, but she wouldn't let me. It wasn't my place to touch her—she belonged to someone else.

SACRED RELIC

SHE POPPED A DVD in the player and turned the channel.

"Hey! I was watching that."

She ignored me, flicking the remote until the title, *Big Booty Bitches,* appeared on the screen. We both knew it was a futile request. She'd get her way. She always did.

"We're gonna play a little game. It's called Mimic." As I watched, she shimmied out of her clothes and tossed them on the floor.

"Press play," she commanded, her heavy breasts hanging in front of my face.

I swallowed heavily, wanting to get to the fun without the nonsense, but I did as asked.

Two women appeared on the screen; one blonde, one redhead.

We watched while they got the necessary plot details out of the way. The blonde hoisted her partner onto the couch, stomach towards the back, and started rubbing her exposed slit.

Meanwhile, my lover's grin was as wide as the Cheshire Cat. "Mimic?"

"Mimic."

I chose to be the blonde, helped her up on the couch, and looked back at the screen. The blonde knelt on the floor, licking her partner from behind. I took up my stance, sighing as my tongue came in contact with her sweet cunt. My nose pressed between her full cheeks as I fucked her hole.

She arched her back, opening herself, readying herself for me to fuck her asshole.

But not yet.

I stopped long enough to see what they were doing onscreen.

The actresses lacked talent. Their cheesy cries grated my nerves, but it made me more determined to show them up, prove what two women could really do.

The blonde eased her finger in the redhead's anus.

My lover steadied her butt, like she knew what was coming even though she couldn't see the screen. I wondered how many times she'd watched this, envying the actresses until she worked up the nerve to show me.

She welcomed my finger, her hungry ass devouring it.

"Lube," she grunted.

I poured the clear liquid over her, working it until my fingers slid in and out as easily as if I had penetrated her pussy. I added another. And then a third.

Feral groans came from her throat as I thrust, but all too soon, the action onscreen had stopped.

The blonde reached for a strand of beads.

I looked around; I didn't see any.

"On the table. Beside the lamp."

A rosary lay where she said, its beads shining innocently from the light.

"Are you serious?"

"Put 'em in me!"

I pushed them in, two by two, until the heavy wooden cross was all that remained.

Turning back to her pussy, I sucked her clit until her body shook from the need to come, and then eased the beads from her hole.

I held her after she'd finished and stroked her as she cried. I told her how sweet she was for sharing her secret with me. She nodded and laughed, clutching the rosary until the cross was imprinted in her palm.

THE UNENLIGHTENED

I CAME TO A WICCAN RETREAT, enticed by the thought of women dancing naked in the forest, pressing their writhing bodies together, feasting from each other's pussies as they searched for divine instruction. At the very least, I expected some cool magic tricks, but when I mentioned this to my friend, she told me I'd been watching too many movies.

Instead, I sat through a lot of praying and chanting, all the while plotting the many ways to make my friend suffer when I spied a woman sitting across from me. She looked like I felt—bored and unenlightened.

We snuck down to the small river on the edge of the property and snuggled together against a tree. She rolled a joint and shared it with me as we listened to the group worship the Goddess.

The longer I smoked, the more convinced I became that my ideas were right to begin with. When I mentioned this to my new friend, she agreed readily and jumped up to start the dance.

"We don't have a fire."

She pursed her lips, then gathered some leaves and sticks and threw a match until we had a burning blaze.

I pulled off my clothes, so glad to be rid of them. They had become an oppressive weight on my skin. We jumped around our fire, singing and yelling, certain the spirit of one of the earthly spirits had filled our bodies.

Other faces flashed in my subconscious and I realized other women were standing at the edge of the trees to watch our joyful moment.

We didn't stop, but waved them over. "Join us!"

And then there were lots of women, a myriad of bouncing flesh surrounding the fire.

I found my partner in crime and pulled her to our tree. There, we tasted each other's juices, her pussy hovering over my face. Only the strength of my shaky arms kept her from collapsing on top of me.

Woman scent was everywhere. Someone's hands caressed my head, lifting me up so I didn't have to strain my neck.

My first orgasm didn't leave me sated—nowhere close. I disentangled myself and tugged at the hands that had cradled me until her breasts loomed over my face and dipped into my waiting mouth.

She began to rock. I heard a murmur from behind and knew someone had claimed her pussy. Another mouth latched onto me, making it hard to concentrate. I probably bit her nipple harder than I meant to, but from the way she jerked towards me, I figured she welcomed the pain.

Finally, I came, really came, surrounded by all the women and their lust.

I sprawled away from the action and collapsed on the side, content that somehow, I'd found the Goddess after all.

LES TRIUMPHANTES

LARA ZIELINSKY

CONNIE ROOK LEANED with outward nonchalance on the railing of an eighty-foot, two-deck party boat, a plastic champagne flute cupped in her hands. Alternately she looked at the sky blazing with reddish purple streaks of light and the sunset's reflection in the rippling and dark waters of the river.

Relieved she had finished her work in time and been able to make the trip, Connie had met Val an hour before at a small port building. Val had told her she would have a "fantastic" time, then led her through a short maze of the other buildings on the docks and up onto the gangway for the boat, *Les Triumphantes.*

Connie made her way into the throng of women already aboard. Tossed a few greetings, she had been pleased, after looking around at the other women, to realize she had chosen the proper level of attire, business informal. She wore a peach V-neck sweater, her throat accentuated with a single silver chain, and long white slacks with closed-toe white sandals.

There was a buffet set up on the lower deck. One half of the large area was a dance floor. On the other half guests circled around a drink bar. She found herself awkwardly moving from conversation to conversation, frequently listening in, but finding little of interest to chime in, or feeling her own thoughts might be unwelcome.

Maybe I should've stuck with Val, Connie thought. But the other woman, though at first introducing Connie around, had quickly hooked up for the weekend. Connie could see her enjoying attention from a curvy Latina. The looks Connie had received were clearly of the "you-should-move-on" variety. Val had only offered a distracted "Have a good time" as Connie moved to the small bar and requested the special she had heard the woman in front of her order, a drink full of swirling color the bartender had called a "Rainbow Sunrise." She nodded her thanks, paid her money, and escaped to the top deck.

The top deck was open and breezy, and populated mostly by couples. The pairs of women walked leisurely around the deck engrossed in quiet, intimate conversations. She had made eye contact with a few, but no one moved to talk to her.

Maybe I'm just not cut out for this, Connie thought sullenly. Dating wasn't a problem usually. It was the unattached searching between that she could do without. She tended, she realized, to stumble over her prospects. Brad, Michael, Harry, Josh, and, she admitted, definitely Kate. She inhaled sharply—the mind-blowing first-time experience with the woman was seldom far from her thoughts. The whole reason she had come on this all-woman cruise was to figure out what would happen next.

Did she even know the games? Solemnly she downed the remains of her drink and studied the refracting moonlight through the curved surface.

"Hello."

Connie turned her head to see a woman with brown curly hair in a ponytail. She wore a half-smile under light brown eyes. Her outfit was a braided blue wool turtleneck and dark blue, perhaps even black, slim-fit jeans and cross-trainer athletic shoes. Connie had seen almost no jeans among the attendees and wondered at the woman's choice. Then she noticed the woman looked a bit younger than most of the other cruisers, probably not yet thirty years old.

Returning her gaze to the woman's face, Connie was surprised to see the woman's smile had widened. "Hello," Connie finally replied.

"Do you do that to everyone?" the woman asked.

"What?"

"Frisk them with your eyes." The woman held open her arms, palms facing toward Connie. "No weapons." She then hooked her thumbs onto the edges of her jean pockets.

She seemed to be waiting for a response, but Connie suddenly was at a loss, disarmed by the suggestion she was unapproachable. "I . . . um, I'm sorry. I didn't realize I was . . . doing that," she finished lamely.

The woman's smile returned slowly and Connie found herself watching the mobile and expressive face with interest. *What would she say next?*

"You've got something of a 'deer-in-headlights' look about you a lot of the time." Connie's eyes widened. She looked afraid. "I've seen you at the Midway Club," the other woman explained. "Val invited you on the cruise, right?"

Connie nodded.

"Slept with her yet?"

Connie blinked, again disarmed, and shook her head. "We've talked. I'm not her type."

"She yours?"

"My type? No, I . . ." Connie closed her eyes briefly and as she opened them again, admitted, "I don't know that I have a type." She decided to turn the tables, a bit defensive in her discomfort. "You?"

Her companion leaned backward against the railing, bracing against the surface with her forearms, hands now crossed over her stomach. "Women who like to have fun." Brown eyes lifted, and an eyebrow rose further to accentuate the coming question. "Do you?"

"Within reason, I guess," Connie replied. "What do you like to do?"

"I play softball on the Rainbow league, and I scull for Harvard's squad."

Connie smiled. "I graduated Harvard Law."

"Do any sports?"

"A little running." Connie tried to turn the conversation. "What are you studying at Harvard?"

"Pretty dry stuff," the other woman skirted.

"I'm curious." Connie was surprised to note she truly was curious. She turned toward the other woman, leaning on the railing now with one elbow, and that lowered her height just enough to bring her to eye level with her companion.

Answering with a very dry tone, as if to say, "I'm going to regret this," the woman did answer. "I'm a fourth-year student in biomedical engineering."

Connie, however, was no intellectual slouch, and did at least know one hot topic to which that field of study could apply. "Are you in stem cell research?"

"No. Gene therapy." Her insight paid off when her companion smiled. "Particularly disease therapy. I'm impressed. Most people's eyes glaze over."

Connie decided that warranted granting the woman her name. "My name's Connie."

"I'm Elizabeth. What do you do?"

Now it was Connie's turn to expect a poor reaction. "Promise me no pity looks?"

"Hey, would I do that?"

Connie then answered the question. "I'm a high school teacher."

"With a law degree?"

She sighed. There was that surprise again. "I practiced corporate law for a while. I like teaching more."

"Yeah, but comparatively speaking, the pay's pretty much crap."

Connie nodded. "Yeah, and your point? I imagine you're not studying all those medical concepts strictly for the money, either."

Elizabeth blinked. "Bleeding heart here," she admitted. "I'm actually looking forward to clinicals. Most of my classmates want to stay in the lab."

"Which disease are you most focused on?"

"Cancer."

Connie looked off at the water, suddenly surprised by how her memory and emotions wrestled with the singular word.

"Hey?" Elizabeth's hand brushed Connie's wrist.

"Sorry. I haven't . . . thought about that in a long time."

Apparently Elizabeth was familiar with the reaction. Insightfully she asked, "Relative?"

Connie exhaled. "My grandmother. Breast cancer."

"It's hereditary, you know. Do you get regular exams?" Connie looked surprised. Elizabeth was contrite. "Hey, sorry, doctor in me blurting out there. I'll poke her back to silence."

Connie let her smile come back. "I need a refill," she said finally. "Come down with me to get another drink?"

◆

BY MIDNIGHT, *Les Triumphantes* floated in the relatively open waters of Massachusetts Bay. Connie only realized the time, though, when the sound of bells drifted across the quiet waters from one of the many land points shrouded in haze. She and Elizabeth had retrieved second, third, and fourth drinks together. The younger woman encouraged Connie to try a fuzzy navel, and then a drink whose name she couldn't recall, which tasted distinctly of butterscotch.

Connie saw couples ducking into a doorway along the wall she and Elizabeth were leaning against, sitting on the deck looking out over the gently lapping waves. Connie had assumed the wall belonged to the wheelhouse, location of the captain and navigational equipment. Now she wasn't so sure. She nudged Elizabeth's shoulder, as the younger woman had been looking off in the direction of the midnight bells. "Do you want to go inside?" She indicated where another couple were just moving out of view.

Elizabeth looked at their twin positions, sitting on the deck, backs up against the wall. Had Connie not rubbed her shoulder, the two wouldn't be in contact at all. Each had her free arm wrapped around a bent knee. "I didn't think you were interested," she said.

The light bulb went on, and Connie blushed. "You mean . . . ?"

"This *is* a party boat." Connie looked again at the doorway. "Wanna see who's playing tonight?" Elizabeth was suddenly on her feet, discreetly adjusting the crotch of her jeans before offering Connie a hand up. "Come on."

The door was only a few feet away now. Feeling absurd, Connie almost closed her eyes as Elizabeth led her through the door. Almost. She was too curious quite to manage it.

First she noticed women seemed to cover every available surface. All the couches, chairs, low tables, and the floor had women on them. Some were in various states of undress and nuzzling with a neighbor. Most, however, watched the 52–inch projection television set on the far wall. It took a change in camera angle for Connie to identify a pair of women onscreen, in the throes of passionate lovemaking.

Elizabeth found them seats on the floor, and Connie sat, cross-legged at first, eyes roaming the actresses' figures.

One woman was a blonde, the other a brunette, and the editing was tasteful. The contact and dialogue were about connection and devotion more than sex, though Connie did catch a few appreciative noises from the audience when a long-fingered hand slipped down the taut muscles of a fit, feminine stomach.

Her own stomach muscles jumped in response. Elizabeth's voice rumbled against her ear. "Giving you any ideas?"

Connie nodded; Elizabeth's lips brushed the left side of her throat. *Yeah*, she thought. *It's giving me an idea just how clueless I am.*

But I want to know, she admitted. Letting the alcohol bolster her bravery, she turned her gaze from the mesmerizing images and tilted her head down to meet Elizabeth's lips.

The soft, sweetly alcohol-flavored lips coaxed open her own. She inhaled, and Elizabeth broke the kiss. The younger woman asked quietly, "Want a more private spot?"

Connie provided the answer with a second, shorter kiss, raw with the passion beginning to fill her. Cupping a soft cheek briefly, she nodded. Elizabeth stood again, leading her to a doorway and down the stairs behind it.

Two flights down they emerged into a corridor lined with doors.

Elizabeth pulled out a flat card from her rear jeans pocket and slid it into a lock which briefly flashed a green LED. The knob gave way in her hand, and she gestured for Connie to enter first.

Barely ten by ten, the room held a queen-sized bed and a small nightstand with a wash basin on top. Over on the wall was a small porthole through which Connie saw the tops of waves.

"We're under the dance deck," Elizabeth explained, coming up behind Connie and using her body to cradle the taller woman's back. The contact, warm and erotic as Elizabeth slightly ground her crotch into Connie's rear, ignited the alcohol in Connie's blood. "Do you want to know what it can really be like, baby?"

Caught in something of a haze, the teacher nevertheless welcomed the opportunity to be the student.

◆

ELIZABETH WAS TALKATIVE, occasionally vulgar, but extremely instructive for Connie. She discovered what she had previously categorized, from her heterosexual experiences, as the all-too-brief foreplay could and did bring orgasms all on its own.

Not a fan of penetration, Elizabeth declined when Connie attempted it. Connie was used to the hurried nature of most of her male partners. But Elizabeth only urged her to "give me some tongue action." To Connie's surprise Elizabeth orgasmed several times. Yet she was ready to go again quickly, urging Connie around and settling between her thighs to return the favor.

It was the first time Connie recalled achieving orgasm without something inside for her spasming muscles to hold. Even climax with Kate had only come once either of them had used fingers. The sensation felt as though a dozen birds were inside her, their wings fluttering against her stomach and groin. She shook and screamed. Elizabeth's tongue continued stroking her on through several smaller waves, and finally to rest.

Connie flung her arm over her eyes. Even the shadowed room seemed suddenly too bright, and her eyes watered. She had no idea she could come that hard.

Elizabeth's gradual glide up her body, further sensitizing bits of flesh with tiny nipping kisses, had Connie almost fully aroused again by the time the firmly muscled body settled against hers. A soft thigh rubbed her groin, and she found herself rocking into the pleasure. "Oh, God," Connie panted.

Elizabeth moved her arm away then, giggling at Connie's dazed expression. Combining deep tongue kisses with her rocking body, she soon had Connie throbbing on the brink of orgasm again.

"Good, huh?"

Connie blinked. "Now I understand the term 'white bread sex.' I never realized . . ."

Elizabeth dipped her head and mouthed Connie's left nipple, teasing it with her teeth. "The guys just spent long enough to warm themselves up, huh?"

"I used to think five minutes was good."

"We've been at it about an hour," Elizabeth surprised her. "I hope though you don't think I'm done." The collegian grinned. "I'm just getting started. Your body is incredible."

Elizabeth stroked down from Connie's right nipple and scratched erotically through the hair covering Connie's sex. "If you're still wet in another hour—" Connie's eyes widened. "I'll bring out Charlie to finish you off."

"Charlie?"

"Check the nightstand drawer," Elizabeth answered.

Connie rolled over and, while Elizabeth fit her pelvis against her rear, opened the drawer. Inside she gazed in surprise at a neon pink vibrator with an attached control for speed adjustment. She squirmed and Elizabeth's fingers slipped against her labia from behind.

A throaty laugh as the fingers withdrew told Connie her reaction had not gone unnoticed. Lips began kissing down the back of Connie's shoulder. "I'm going to make you laugh at the next man who thinks he can satisfy you." The laughter rolled over Connie, as she was rolled onto her stomach and nipping kisses covered her rear. She pushed her ass up and clutched the sheets as Elizabeth's mouth found her clitoris from underneath. "Oh, God," Connie breathed, inhaling the pure pleasure.

◆

"ELIZABETH" QUICKLY DEVOLVED to "Beth" for the continually aroused Connie. Attention to detail did not begin to describe Beth's devotion to seeking out and exploiting every millimeter of Connie's intimate flesh—and some not so intimate. Connie groaned and panted appreciatively as Beth currently had Connie on her stomach while fluttering her tongue in the hollow between bone and muscle at the back of Connie's knees.

Connie found the possessiveness utterly enthralling and she was still wet and hungry when Beth slipped a finger again inside her sex. "More?" Beth asked. Her hot breath tickled the back of Connie's damp neck as her groin rotated provocatively against Connie's rear.

All Connie could do was beg, "Oh, God, yes."

"Good. Now." Beth paused and rolled her body over Connie's, igniting nerve endings everywhere her breasts or mound hairs brushed against her body. Connie felt like she could make love forever. "I want you to pay attention to everything I'm going to do to you. No man will ever pay this kind of attention to your pleasure." Having already learned Connie's instant-rocket reactions to coarse language, Beth slowly wiggled two fingers inside Connie's expectant channel and cooed, "Your cunt is pure velvet."

Because her vaginal walls fluttered sharply at the evocative words, Connie felt every twitch as the two fingers, moving alternately together and separately, seemed intent to crawl right into her belly. "Oh, God," she groaned, arched, and panted again.

"Yeah, like a glove," Beth added. Keeping her fingers inside Connie, Beth coaxed her onto her back. The flutters continued and Connie could not help rocking, arching, gasping as her belly muscles clenched and unclenched rhythmically. She moaned with pleasure as Beth's thumb gently flicked in time over her clit to the pulsations filling her stomach.

While Connie watched, leaning back on her elbows, the brown-haired woman leaned forward while continuing to hold Connie's gaze. When her face was a few inches away from Connie's, Beth dropped her gaze, then her head, to suck abruptly and hard on Connie's rock-hard right nipple.

Connie lurched upward and Beth's fingers began stroking again, this time in rhythm with her sucking on Connie's nipples, first right, then left. Connie's moans soon joined the rhythm and she became disconnected from everything except the fingers inside her, the hot, wet mouth around her nipples, and the soft hair in her hands as she stroked Beth's head.

She felt when Beth introduced a third finger, and her inner walls rippled and released. She threw her head back, moaning and panting for more.

On the edge of her perception, Connie saw Beth reach over and open the drawer. Her entire body convulsed on one excited thought: *Charlie*.

She felt her juices flowing out around Beth's fingers and grinned as she heard the buzz start near her right ear. She opened her eyes and turned toward the thick phallic toy, able to discern the slight blur of its movement.

It lowered slowly and Beth brushed it lightly across her still-hard nipples, laughing throatily when Connie arched her back, further thrusting out her breasts. Beth engulfed the left nipple, then chewed on the skin surrounding the teat while letting the phallus drift down Connie's stomach; her abdominals quaked in anticipation.

When the buzzing toy first brushed up against the inside of Connie's right thigh, Connie tried to close her thighs and capture its vibration against her skin.

"I have loads more control than some guy only thinking with his dick, Connie," Beth whispered, then kissed Connie as she brushed their nipples together, sending a jolt of pure fire to Connie's groin, where the tip of the phallus was just brushing across the wet outer folds of Connie's sex.

Then Beth began a patient, teasing penetration. Connie almost went insane with the bulbous head dipping, stroking, retreating, and, all the while, vibrating with a slow, heartlike throb.

It was about halfway in when her hips surged forward. Beth moved down, told Connie to lean back, and sucked Connie's clit between her teeth as she pushed the vibrator all the way in.

"Fuck!" After the slow buildup, to be suddenly full, Connie nearly soared into orgasm right that second. "Oh, God . . . yes," she moaned as Beth plied the tip of her clit with her tongue, wiggling it between her teeth. She felt every vibration in her bones as Beth chuckled against her skin. She reached between her thighs and bent her knees higher, opening herself and rocking into Beth's motions.

Over and over again she moved, and then she continued through while her body crested on wave after wave of orgasm. Beth's tongue moved in and around the dildo, lapping up juices while Connie continued to come.

Eyes closed, Connie felt Beth settle over her, their breasts pillowing together. The dildo rested, still vibrating, between their bellies as Beth rocked their pelvises together.

Connie reached down, cupped Beth's buttocks, and wrapped her legs around behind Beth's knees.

That brought their sexes into direct contact. Beth's labia fluttering against Connie's sent the younger woman into orgasm.

Connie felt the little drops, warm and silky, slip out of Beth and wet her own mound.

Using her right hand to cup Beth's left breast, Connie guided the nipple above her to her mouth and sucked, sustaining Beth's orgasm for several further seconds until the woman collapsed against her.

The dildo rolled away, forgotten, and Connie rolled over Beth, sliding her fingers into Beth's folds to feel, and extend, the rippling continuing in her wet, hot center.

LOVE LETTER

MIEL ROSE

YOU'VE BEEN IN MY THOUGHTS so much lately. Waking and sleeping, though most mornings I can't remember my dreams. When I wake up it's like you were just in bed with me, like maybe you're in the bathroom down the hall instead of an ex I haven't seen for years. And when I leave my house for the day I keep mistaking people for you walking down the street. It's like you're hovering in my peripheral vision; if I turn my head fast enough maybe I'll catch you.

Where are you? I know it's a little late in the game, but you being on my mind so much brings up this idea of fate and how often we used to talk about destiny in relation to us. That was back when we were so crazy in love we couldn't walk straight. That time is so present with me now and I can't shake this idea that you're about to show up at my door any minute.

There's this old conversation of ours that keeps playing out in my head. I was going through a tough time then, kind of like now, which is probably why I'm thinking about it so much. Who knew your words would still be encouraging me after all this time?

We were on a date and you were making me dinner and I was heart sore over some crazy kind of drama that only exists in small queer communities. It was something I can't even remember now, but at the time it was triggering a whole lot of self-doubt. I felt so drained, like the slightest challenge could make me fold, make me question my strength.

I was trying to explain this to you when you grabbed my chin and looked fiercely into my eyes. "Girl, you are so fucking strong. Don't you ever doubt that. That's the crazy thing about you. Hell, that's the crazy thing about a lot of the femmes I've known. You're as strong as steel, like you could take on anything you had to, and you have, I mean, you do. Somehow that steel doesn't form an edge and cut you inside. Somehow you can still be so vulnerable, and so strong, at the same time."

I gaped at you, shook my head, sure you had it all wrong. You said, "Baby, that's why I love you so goddamn much." You threw your hands up in exasperation, slapping them down on your thighs. "That's what gets me every time, your crazy strength and your vulnerability. I don't know, maybe you'll get pissed when I say this, but that's what makes me want to protect you so much. I've seen way too many people turn hard in my life. It's not like you can't take care of yourself, I *know* you can, but why should you always have to? I mean, fuck! Why should any of us always have to? Why do we do so much fighting alone? Baby, I just want you to know I got your back."

As I remember, it wasn't long after that you rolled me onto that back you wanted to protect, crawled between my legs, and fucked me so sweet for the rest of the night.

It was a continuing theme with us, this concept of how to protect each other in a world that wants us broken or dead. I remember slow dancing with you in this bar, slow dancing even though we could have easily been grinding like everyone else on the floor. We were cheek to cheek, your hands on my hips, my lower back, my nails tracing patterns on your neck, on your shoulders. You whispered in my ear, asked me if I thought you were a misogynist pig. This was because fifteen minutes earlier you had slammed some guy against the wall, your hand on his throat, because he had reached up my skirt when I was walking past. You asked me if I felt like you were trying to fight my fights for me, taking up too much space, being too macho. Your face was hot against mine. I wondered if you were thinking about all the bar fights you used to get into, growing up poor and angry and queer, how you were trying to calm down in your old age of thirty-five years.

Instead of answering you directly, I told you about the time I bitched out this woman I overheard saying how sorry she felt for masculine women, how twisted and wounded they must feel inside. A deep and terrible violence had welled up in me. I tried to stay calm, tried to tell her nicely that she didn't know shit. I wanted to spit in her face, rip her to shreds. This was only partly in defense of you, of all the masculine-gendered, female-born guys I've loved as friends, brothers, or lovers. It was also in defense of me, of my gendered, queer life. You are a piece of me. Not a half to fit mine and make a whole—I'm whole all on my own—but like a piece of my same puzzle. The puzzle that makes up our big, crazy, queer, homo lives. Sometimes fighting each other's fight is the same as fighting our own. Like you said, why should we always have to fight alone? Even if we are on different sides of this circle that makes up queer gender, this circle everyone tries to teach us is a straight line.

You being willing to fight for femmes, you trying so hard to stay on top of the misogyny that threatens to rip us and our community apart, this is what made me powerfully in love with you. The fact that you were the best lover I've ever had was icing on the cake. Mile-high icing that just might have dissolved my teeth if I didn't brush right after.

Metaphor can't really describe it, though, the way you could be so sweet and tender while you fucked me raw from behind, beating my ass until I bruised. The way you could cause me pain so sweet and overwhelming it would have me crying for hours, fighting demons I barely knew I had, until I emerged feeling light, like I had slipped off a backpack full of cement I'd been carrying around for a very long time.

There were so many first times for me with you. The first time I sucked cock and really loved it, it was you who had strapped it on for me. I loved it so much that sometimes I would come just from sucking you. It would make me so hot, the way you would talk to me, tell me how good my lips felt wrapped around your shaft, how skilled my mouth was working you up and down, how sexy I looked with tears running down my cheeks, gagging on your cock as you fucked my face.

It got crazy for a while, like I had caught some kind of cock-sucking fever that left me with bruised and dirty knees. It was after you started packing on a regular basis. You would walk through the door and my eyes would go to your crotch. My mouth would start to water and my knees would just buckle. I had to have your dick in my mouth right there, immediately. I didn't give a fuck if we were in the living room. You would just look down at me, so amused as I frantically unbuttoned your fly, trying to get at you. You'd lean against the nearest wall, grab my hair, and guide your cock out of your pants and into my mouth in smooth slow motion.

How can I explain the strange mix of comfort and lust this produced inside me? The tension in my jaw as I opened to accommodate you, the silky feel of your silicone on my tongue, the panic that was always there the moment your cock head hit the back of my throat, stimulating my stubborn gag reflex. How can I explain how fully I felt your energy, as well as the actual cock, penetrate my mouth, that it was never pantomime, never just imagination? It was your cock I was sucking, your cock slipping into my tight throat, your energetic come shooting into my mouth. That's why I was crazy about it. The cock was YOURS.

You were the key I'd been waiting for. Other guys had tried to figure me out, but I was a mystery even to myself. I played the submissive girl, but there was always something lacking. No one really touched me. I was a master of walls, my internal landscape a labyrinth that I let my lovers wander through, knowing full well they would never find the heart. You had a height and breadth of perception that was shocking. How was it possible to see inside another human being like that? Smooth like cream, you broke me down and laid me out, held me to your light to see what I was made of.

Which might be why I did things with you I wouldn't do with other guys.

You were the first person I let fuck my ass, which was something I'd always reserved for myself. My pussy and I never got along so well, ever since the time I tried to pop my own cherry in isolated queer desperation. Later, I could open to lovers, my muscles relaxing with the need for their big hands shoved up inside my cunt. It never worked the same when I was by myself.

It surprised me when I started experimenting with butt sex alone, how intensely I liked it, how I would get off in record speed. My second surprise was when I quickly surpassed my first butt plug and felt how easy it was to shove three well-lubed fingers up my asshole.

But it wasn't something I could do with someone else. Ass fucking seemed so intimate, so potentially embarrassing. And until you, no one had ever challenged that boundary. You worked me slow and steady, like a glacier on a mountain range, eroding my self-consciousness bit by bit. It's like you had a plan, and you were constantly implementing it.

First, you would give my ass attention any way you could. When I was sore from standing up all day at work, you would give me these rubdowns that always claimed to be full bodied, but somehow always wound up focusing on my butt. After a beating with your hand or your belt, you would cool me down, kissing, licking, and caressing my welts. "Did you bathe today?" became code for "Can I lick your asshole?"

You told me you couldn't care less about messy butt sex, you just wanted to fuck my ass. Finally, you bought me a large bulb syringe to clean out with and a one-and-a-half-inch-diameter butt plug. You even told me that when we used it together I could take the plug out in private afterwards if I needed to. You were such a gentleman.

But the first time you fucked my ass with your cock, it was all my idea.

I knew it was something I wanted and I knew I wanted it from you. And even though you had made it clear you would move mountains to get in my ass, I wanted to make it easy for you. I wanted to gift it to you, wrap this particular virginity in a bow and hand it to you on a platter. So I made the date with you, whispering my intentions in your ear so you would know what was up, so you would come prepared.

My own preparation was also important. If this was a gift to you, it was also a gift to myself, and my ritual of self-love and care had to reflect this. Between the bubble bath and the enema, the most important thing cleansed that day was any lingering fear or shame about what we were about to do.

When you walked into my room that night I was lying on my bed, naked, on my stomach, reading a book. I heard your boots on the stairs and my skin broke out in goose bumps. You walked into my room and I heard you moan low in your throat, seeing me exposed for you. You crossed the floor to my bed and I automatically fell into a game we sometimes played. I ignored you and tried to look like I was interested in my book. I knew it was the right thing to do when you said, "Keep reading."

I didn't even look at you. I twirled a strand of hair around my finger and kept my eyes on my book. You got onto the bed behind me and I felt your hands on my hips, felt your lips trailing kisses across my lower back, down my ass, dangerously close to my crack. I felt your tongue dart out, lick across the line where ass becomes leg, lick towards my center. You spread me open and I moaned. I couldn't help it.

"Shut up, you're supposed to be reading," you said, and ran your tongue across my asshole.

I took a deep breath and tried not to raise my hips up and back them into your face. Your tongue continued to lap at my asshole, circling it, probing with the very tip. You pushed your tongue into my hole and I held myself still, relaxed. You thrust your tongue in and out of my ass, fucking me. You groaned, pulled out, and said, "You're so open, baby," and plunged your tongue back in.

Usually your addressing me directly signified an end to the game, and I took it like this because I couldn't stand being quiet and still anymore. I started rocking back at you and you wrapped your hands around my hips, pulling me into you. You reached under my body and found my clit hard and slippery and so desperate for your attention. I pulled my knees up under my body and thrust my hips back at you hard, told you how much I needed you, how much I wanted you. You grabbed for the lube, squirted it all over your hand, and thrust two thick fingers up my ass. You worked my hole hard and fast, knowing I was ready, that I needed you like that. I leaned back onto your hand, wanting more, fell into your lap, and felt your hard-on against the back of my thigh. You held your hand against your crotch, putting pressure on your dick as you let me fuck myself onto your fingers.

Knowing I needed more, needing more yourself, you slapped my ass and pushed me forward onto the bed. Your fingers slipped out of my hole, making me want to cry. I heard you unzip your fly, I heard the squirt of the lube bottle. I felt the cold of fresh lube on my asshole, and then I felt the pressure of your cock head pushing in.

Just as I had planned, you went in easy. I had stretched my hole earlier, getting ready for you. My muscles relaxed for you and you thrust your cock into my ass, pumping slowly in and out, and then faster as I thrust back at you. You grabbed my hips, holding me still, setting your own pace, running the show. You teased me by slowing down, making me beg for the hard fuck I wanted. You slapped my ass and told me that you had waited so long to get your cock up into this sweet hole that you were going to pace yourself and enjoy it.

It was all bullshit. You were as worked up as I was, and you didn't make me wait long for the hard, fast fuck we both needed. You didn't make me wait long before you snaked your hand under my body and rubbed my clit until I came, screaming, muscles tense around your cock.

I guess the thing that gets me, makes my heart ache, is how much trust there was in our sex. How much I trusted your love, how respected I felt by you. Maybe I had always thought that loving someone like that, with trust and respect, would make sex boring, but our sex was the hottest I've ever had. I went places with you I never thought I could go.

I still don't really understand how so much love and passion could transform into so much anger and resentment, or how I could have lost track of you over the years. I do know that I never quite shook you loose from my heart, and that I still think of you with an aching loss.

Even though I'm always hoping that I'll run into you, I have no idea what I would say. For a while there, so much of our conversations had nothing to do with words, or just used words as a structure for all the feelings that we poured out our eyes at each other. I wonder if we could still communicate like that. I wonder if I packed this whole letter behind my eyes and radiated it out to you, simply saying, "I've missed you," if you would understand.

P.S. I LOVE YOU

KISSA STARLING

NANCY PLACED THE LACY pink stationery on the desk and touched the filigree calligraphy pen to the paper. Her hand shook back and forth. She took a deep breath in through her nose and released it out her mouth. The pen rested against her cheek while she thought about what to write. The yellow, faded letters sat in front of her. They would help her memory and her muse, but she'd have to read them for it to work. One more deep breath and she began to read . . .

August 14, 1969

I got here early. I hitchhiked most of the way. There are a few others here but we're all kind of hiding out in one of the fields across the street. Thanks again for ordering these tickets for me early, John. Eighteen dollars seemed like a lot at the time but now that I'm here it was so worth it. I can see some sort of big machines flattening out the alfalfa. So groovy, wish you were here. Don't worry; I have everything I need in my flower backpack. Who knows? Maybe I'll get lucky!

Peace,

K

August 15, 1969

There are thousands of people here. They're still trying to get in and get parked. Some buses have, like, fifty people in them. Kids are riding on the roof and the hood—anywhere they can get a spot. I can't believe how many people have small children, and they brought them, too. How cool is that? There was this huge chain-link fence that bordered the right side of the farm but I helped push it down. It made it easier for the crowd to get where they wanted to go.

Some are sleeping in vans or tents, but most of us are lying under the stars. I didn't sleep alone last night. I met this beautiful woman named Nancy; I call her Nan. She calls me Kitty. Not sure why but I haven't told her my real name yet. I doubt I'll ever see her again after this weekend so it doesn't matter what I tell her. You're the only one I can talk about my women with; Mom and Dad would have a fit. Your friend Rob took us to the wrong venue to begin with. There we were in Woodstock all by our lonesomes. Some kids drove through and told us the location was changed last month. I guess you didn't know since you were gone and have other things on your mind. I wish you could be here with me.

The music started around four this afternoon. I swooned with everyone else while Richie Havens sang about freedom and the war. The stage wasn't even finished yet and that powerhouse voice boomed out regardless. I know how much you dig John Sebastian. He wasn't on the announcement poster but so many bands were stuck in the traffic jam that he volunteered to strum away on that guitar of his. At the end of his set he told us that we were all beautiful—and we believed him. Sweetwater got up right after that. They were the first band to perform. I told you I'd keep step-by-step notes on everything you're missing. What a blast! Get to feeling better; I hope to see you soon.

Peace,

K

Nancy grinned when she read the name—Kitty. That darn-blasted, sexy gal wouldn't give her real name when they first met, and after a few tokes on a joint she didn't really care what her name was. All she paid attention to was the soft touch of her lips and the smoky smell of her long brown hair, and the way her fingers traveled under her shorts and along her inner thigh towards her center. They were oblivious to the world when their bodies wiggled beneath the thread-worn sleeping bag made for one. Not even the warm, sticky night air or smell of cow manure forced them out. They'd come to Bethel, New York, to live free and feel good about themselves, and that's exactly what they did.

Their first time together held surprise and exploration. Nancy still recalled their first kiss. It was behind a tree on the edge of the field. She'd been the one to tilt towards Katherine with her eyes closed. The pair touched their closed lips together for a few puckered moments and then their tongues explored the inside of each others' mouths. Katherine smelled, and tasted, of black licorice. Nancy still ate the stuff even though she detested the horrid flavor. It reminded her of their first kiss.

Katherine always did have a nipple fetish. She'd sucked Nancy's tits for hours on end. Her fingers rubbed the outside of her panties the whole time. God, what ecstasy. She remembered how her body was stretched out like a fine-tuned guitar when that girl stuck her warm, wet tongue inside of her pussy. Juices ran between her legs as the tip of her new best friend tantalized her clit. The fact that people watched the two of them together had only excited Nancy more. Both of them came with a quiet yell and a round of applause. Public sex was common back then. Funny—they never grew out of that phase; it just became more taboo as society *evolved.*

They'd awakened with the sunrise the next morning; well, Nancy had. She'd left Kitty to sleep and toured the festival grounds. Girls and guys slept everywhere. There wasn't a bare spot as far as she saw. It amazed her that Sam's dad had let the festival take place on his farm. They went to school together and Sam had invited her to the festival. He hadn't known at the time that she preferred chicks to dicks. His tall, lanky body lay next to some barefoot blonde who was half dressed with a simple smile on her face and beads around her neck. At least he wasn't alone.

The makeshift, meager stage held a few leftover instruments. It looked as if a few groupies had thrown their handmade maracas and tambourines up there. What a wild night it had been. Thousands sang, danced, and made out while Joan Baez rocked the party out. The goddess, Joan. To this day Nan couldn't believe she'd had a conversation with Joan Baez out in a field, in the middle of a farm, in Bethel, New York. It was an unforgettable part of her history—her life. Even if it was just "Hi."

She picked up the next letter and unfolded it with great care.

August 16, 1969

I can't believe I'm still here. This is the most awesome time I've had in my entire life. Wow, man, everyone's so nice here. Nan and I got down and dirty last night. No lesbian-haters here as far as I can tell. People were grunting and banging all around us. The sounds made me even hotter for my new gal-pal. We swayed to the music with our arms in the air last night until the wee hours of the morning, and then we lay naked on top of some dingy, polyester bag she carries around with her. We were plenty warm 'cause we lay real close, if you know what I mean.

The music doesn't start until later in the afternoons, so we sleep late, make love, and swim nude in the water nearby. We aren't ever alone there, but neither of us is bothered by the other nude nature lovers. I've seen bongs made from aluminum foil and a flag with the peace symbol used instead of stars. The usual oppressions of life aren't here with us for the weekend. People sit around and really talk and some pull out their own instruments and sing or play. They chat about how we're stars and we hold the future in our hands—better us than our baby-killing government. Sorry, John, I know you don't like that kind of talk, but it's how I feel.

I wonder how some of these people got here. There's not

enough cars and vans to hold all of 'em. I'm just glad I got to pee in private this morning. Most of the others were out foraging for food by the time I got up. Some pervert was looking at my tits when I opened my eyes. I just jiggled them, sat up, and laughed. He knew I was off-limits when Nan stood in front of me. People here aren't worried about clothing or other material things. I'm joining right in. If it feels good I'm doing it. I saw three naked children beating on a drum set this morning. How wonderful to feel so free.

Peace,

K

Kitty attracted them all. Her sweet smile and innocent eyes had everyone at the festival hooked. Nancy would have beaten them off with a stick, but it wouldn't have done any good. Her girl was natural bait for horny guys and girls alike. She remembered a guy in a dark green army jacket. He was jacked up on something more sinister than pot. There was an evil look in that man's eyes. When he reached for Kitty's tits Nancy slapped him right in the face. Shock showed on his face, and then anger. Two burly guys pulled him away from them, and luckily he didn't show up again for the rest of the festival.

The second night of partying was Nancy's favorite. Janis Joplin was the queen. She stood before all of them with her long vest, beads, and flat brown hair, and sang to them about dreams. What an incredible woman she was. Lighters flickered all over that alfalfa field when she finished her songs. It poured rain by the time the Grateful Dead took the stage. Kitty knew every word to every song they sang that night. Rhythms and melodies danced in their heads hours after the last tunes. The second evening found the two of them fucking on top of the sleeping bag. No inhibitions after that round of music. The sixty-nine position was new to both of them, but they perfected it under a clear night sky. Kitty claimed she didn't know how to lick a woman right, but her tongue delved into places that Nancy didn't know she had. Two flattened love muscles hit the G-spots at the same precise moment and caused both women to come simultaneously. It was the beginning of many such sessions during the weekend.

They'd held one another on the third night while they listened to farmer Max Yasgur give a speech to the huge crowd. It took forever for him to get his words out. People screamed, cheered, and even clapped after he spoke only a short sentence. Time and time again he paused to let the noise lower. He'd praised them for being the largest group ever assembled in one place. They were there to change the world through music. His words gave them power.

That night they cut their palms with a broken beer bottle and shook hands. They were blood sisters. That was the night they knew it was love. Nan wondered what they ever did with that power? Had they made a difference? Would anyone notice when they were both gone?

They missed Jimi Hendrix on the last day. She later heard that the crowd of five hundred thousand dwindled to only thirty-five thousand by the time the famous icon took the stage. It hadn't messed his career up as far as she saw. He was still known as the best guitarist ever.

Tomorrow Nancy planned to stand on Max Yasgur's six-hundred-acre farm and view his grave. He'd died only four years after the infamous music festival, and new owners watched over it now. Many tried to revive the energy of the original Woodstock, but ultimately they all failed.

◆

NANCY ROSE to the incessant beep of an alarm. She hated to wake up in strange rooms, in a bed that wasn't her own. The aluminum walker assisted her to an upright stance. It was mental torture to use the darn thing, but two early hip replacements made it a necessary evil. That which took her only a few minutes on a normal day took her much longer today. Her dentures soaked to a gleaming white overnight. Lord, how she wished she'd taken better care of her teeth. A stiff pouf of hair sat atop her head. Those weekly appointments with the hairdressers made things easier for her. She cringed when her arthritic hand reached for the knit pullover top. No buttons here. Why couldn't she have gotten the genes of an athlete instead of an aging accountant? Old age equaled hell. A knock on the door startled her.

"Are you ready yet, Aunt Nan?" Such a sweet boy, her nephew. One of her brother's sons. He'd agreed to come along for her final journey to Mecca.

"I'll be right down, Harris. Why don't you pull the car around?"

She needed a few moments alone before they left. They'd made this journey so many times in the last fifty years. Nan remembered their trip last year . . .

"Nan, do you remember this? We sat on top of the concession stand after they ran out of food. We had the best seat in the house. This is the spot where we first kissed. I was so scared back then. I didn't want you to know I was a virgin lesbian, or girlgin as the lesbians these days call it."

A tear trickled down Nan's cheek. Good memories. It brought

both of them happiness each year to come back here and relive one of the best times of their lives.

The small yellow jar fit in her purse. One lift at a time and her feet slipped into the shoes by the end of the bed. It was time to go. At the last minute Nancy picked up the scented envelope from the desk and dropped it into her purse alongside the decorative jar. Four touches—one each to her forehead, chest, and each shoulder—gave her the courage to continue on. *In the name of the Father, the Son, and the Holy Ghost.*

◆

"WE'RE HERE, Aunt Nan. Should I get out with you?"

"I'll just stand right next to the door, thank you. Pull up close to that grave right there. I'll let you know if I need your assistance."

Ahavath Israel Cemetery was a bleak place and she didn't plan to stay long. "Thank you, Mr. Yasgur. It was because of you that I met the love of my life. We both thank you."

Nancy touched the headstone briefly but didn't let go of the car door. After a short, silent prayer she slipped into the seat. "Last stop—Woodstock."

Harris shifted the car into gear without a word, and for that Nancy was happy. They rode in silence for a few short miles to the old Yasgur farm. He pulled over to the side and stopped. When the car was shut off he stepped out and placed a lawn chair out in the field.

This time she looped the massive black purse over her arm and used the walker that Harris removed from the trunk. "Take as much time as you need, Aunt Nan. Wave if you need me. I'll be in the car."

It took every bit of five whole minutes to get to the perfect spot, but she made it on her own. That was an accomplishment these days. The chair creaked a bit from her weight and the feet sank into the soft ground. This was it; there was no more time for delay. Katherine had kept the letters since her brother died in Vietnam. The army forwarded all of his personal belongings to her. How surprised she'd been that he kept all of their correspondence. Nancy pulled the last letter from her pants pocket.

August 17, 1969

The system sure is bringing us down. I know that now. I wish I could stay here forever, just like this. What a bummer to have to leave. Most of the concession stands ran out of food early yesterday, but who cares? Lots of people are making huge pots of food and sharing it. We should run this country—all we need is to be free.

Funny how their concept of freedom changed with time—and loss. John died for his country, and that single act turned Katherine's views around. It became a way to honor her brother's memory, and it was the one issue in their lives that spiked debate up until the last breath of her beautiful lover. Nancy read on . . .

This crazy freak of a girl just told me she was headed home. I didn't mean to tell her how I felt, but I do love her. It may have been the doobie talking. You may not think it's possible after only a few days, to love someone, but it is. We're closer than any two people have ever been in the his-

tory of our country. I'm going with her. I don't know for sure where she's going, but I'm going, too. I wanted to see Jimi Hendrix, but it doesn't seem that I will on this trip. I'm sure we'll come back next year and maybe even every year after that. I officially declare this our anniversary date, August seventeenth. This is the place where I dawned a new day, and this is the place I'll come back to when I die. I miss you so much, John. You would love my new girlfriend. Yes, I said it—girlfriend. (This is me sticking my tongue out at you!) Heal those legs and get home as fast as you can.

Nan and Kitty forever . . .

Peace,

K

They'd both slowed down on the Mary Jane as they'd grown older, but neither of them quit completely. They lived through the Kennedy assassination, Vietnam, and Evel Knievel's attempt to jump the canyon. The two of them saw an actor become president and same-sex marriages become legal—in some places, anyway. Together, through it all, their love never once faltered.

They'd talked about what would happen at the end. Neither of them was afraid of death—only of being alone. Nancy removed the jar from her purse and loosened the lid. A slow breeze swept in front of her, and that's when she emptied the contents of her vessel. With great care she laid the jar on the ground in front of her and pulled her final letter from her purse.

August 17, 2008

My dear-sweet, Katherine,

This is the place I first laid eyes on you with your braided hair and faded-denim shorts. The yellow ribbon entwined in your locks that day became my salvation. You don't know that I carried it with me always, but I did. I even bought a yellow urn to hold your ashes. We made sweet love and mingled our own blood that weekend. Something worked because we never parted since that day. I think we made our own magic.

I won't go on much longer alone. We discussed that, I know. I'm not trying to be morbid, but there's nothing here for me without your touch, your voice, your love . . . I've traveled all this way to fulfill the promise I made to you. Your ashes are spread on the ground of our Mecca—the place we drove to year after countless year to celebrate our anniversaries of love. This is the last time I will visit this place. It means nothing without you by my side. Wait for me, my sexy darling. I plan to kiss you all over when we meet again.

Nan

Their initials were drawn inside of a shakily drawn heart complete with an arrow.

Tears ran down Nancy's face. It was too hard, this promise she'd made. When she leaned forward to grieve her knees gave way and she fell, face forward, onto the ground. She heard the car door slam and then someone running towards her.

Harris held her elbow and helped her to stand. Nancy dropped the letter and watched it flutter to the ground. She would leave the urn there in the dirt. Only the bottom of the letter showed. Three fingers on her right hand came to her lips and she mouthed the last words as her nephew guided her away.

P.S. I love you.

RACKULA

HEATHER TOWNE

UPON MY EIGHTEENTH BIRTHDAY, when I became a woman in the jaundiced eyes of Romanian law, my mother sat me down in the musty living room of our ancient cottage and told me the story of the Countess Sabrina Comaneci—the evil, vengeful, undead, large-breasted seductress who haunted the backwoods byways of our impoverished province, deflowering virgins with her serpentlike tongue and jagged fangs, and then hungrily supping on blood from the rents she'd made in the young women's maidenheads.

A single flickering tallow candle illuminated our sparsely furnished parlor, as a violent wind howled around the rotted eaves of our humble abode and twisted tree limbs clawed at the clapping shutters, as if seeking entry. "Her beauty is incandescent, irresistible, the stuff of the great artists Grigorescu and Luchian," my mother intoned. "Women cannot resist her, and men detest her. It is legend that on a night many, many centuries ago, when the evening star Venus was at its zenith, the lust-crazed countess succeeded in seducing one of her kitchen servants, a pretty, virginal girl of eighteen who had only that morning become betrothed to a peasant boy who had courted her for years.

"The countess maneuvered the girl onto her feather bed, then in between her legs. And as she was guiding the young woman's head, her inexperienced tongue, up and down on her brazen sex, just as the countess was teetering on the very edge of ecstasy, great, bold breasts heaving with imminent, explosive release, the young woman's fiancé suddenly rushed into the room, attracted by the animal moaning. And when he beheld the sapphic scene before him, he seized a saber down from the wall and, in a fit of jealous rage, plunged the sword deep into the countess, piercing her wicked heart, slaying the beautiful temptress before she could attain sexual fulfillment.

"And from that night onward, whenever the planet Venus is in its ascension, the countess walks the earth, stalking this province's virgin daughters recently turned eighteen, seeking the ecstasy in death she was denied in life, evilly robbing the men of our land of the honor of deflowering their women. And by taking her fiendish vengeance, temporarily satiating her unquenchable, ages-old lust, she also takes the very life of the young woman she violates. That poor girl becomes a part of the countess's army of the damned, to be used and abused by her for all of eternity."

I stared into my mother's watery blue eyes, at her trembling blue lips, and a cold and clammy shiver traversed the length of my spine. "How can I avoid such a fate, Mama?" I queried.

"By remaining safely and securely locked indoors when Venus is the brightest star in the sky; by never setting foot outside when the countess is on the prowl," she replied, grasping my hands in her bony claws. "Promise me this, oh lovely daughter of mine!"

I earnestly promised to abide by the old woman's superstitious wishes, seeking to reassure her. "And where is Venus now, Mama?" I further inquired.

"In its ascension!" she shrieked, staring fearfully out the dusty window at the darkening sky.

I would have been wise to have heeded my mother's warning, but I was young and foolish and daring, and dubious of Mama's many tall tales and handed-down myths. More importantly, my drop-dead gorgeous, breast-blessed girlfriend, Daria, had promised me a special treat for my birthday, and what come-of-age girl-lover can resist such a titillating vow as that. So, once my mother had retired to the slumbers of her bed, out into the windswept night I ventured.

◆

DARIA AND I RENDEZVOUSED at our usual spot on the mossy green banks of the thin trickle of a cold, clear stream that flowed past an abandoned flour mill. The long shadows of dusk had been usurped by the inky blackness of night, and I kindled to life a small fire, admiring sweet, well-endowed Daria in the glow of its embers.

"You are truly beautiful," I marveled, eyes roaming all over the girl's voluptuous body. I'd been a tit-woman from as far back as memory permits me, and Daria's tremendous bosom was fantastically showcased in a thin, white, clingy summer dress. Her chestnut hair cascaded long and thick over her bare, buff shoulders, and her big brown eyes reflected the dancing flames from the fire, from my eyes, her pretty face shining like a princess's on her wedding night.

"Thank you, Velda," she responded, gazing bashfully into the fire for a moment, and then more assertively back up at me. "I told you I had a special treat for your birthday . . . and here it is." She fumbled the buttons open on the front of her dress, her sparkling eyes locked on mine, and the almost-sheer garment slid down her curvy body with barely a whisper, puddling at her feet, leaving her breathtakingly, stunningly naked!

"Daria!" I breathed, staring in awe at her lush, creamy white body, counting my blessings that the striking girl had finally given in to my entreaties, revealing herself to be in sync with my sexual thinking.

Her breasts were ponderously large, round and ivory, peaked by twin kitten-pink nipples that jutted out a fair half an inch or more from her dewy tit-flesh. And between her smooth, slim legs lay a triangle of downy brown fur—nirvana! When she shifted her legs yet wider apart, I glimpsed the hidden pink of her pussy lips, glistening with moisture and anticipation.

"Daria!" I repeated, overwhelmed, rushing round the fire and into her open arms.

We embraced as long-lost lovers embrace, mashing our lips together, Daria's enormous breasts pressing hotly into my breasts, my nimble hands gripping and squeezing her plump, rounded bottom. We bumped tongues, swirling our slippery pink pleasure appendages together, the two of us fiercely frenching for what seemed like forever. When I at last broke mouth and tongue contact with the drooling girl whom I had lusted after for so, so many years, I commenced kissing and licking and biting my way down her long, slender neck, all the way down to the awesome chest that was the spectacular heritage of all of the women in her blessed family.

I cupped her immense boobs in my covetous hands, reveling in the solid weight and silky, superheated texture of them, and then I bent my head down and licked at one of her rigid nipples, teasing the pebbled underside of it with my flicking tongue. She cried out with pleasure, clutching at my golden hair with her long, sharp-tipped fingers, and I took the fully flowered nipple into my mouth and tugged anxiously on it.

"God, yes, Velda! Suck my tits!" she wailed, amber eyes closed and delicate head lolling back on her shoulders, mountainous breasts and rubbery buds quite obviously super-sensitive to the touch.

I suckled her swollen nipples like a hungry baby, then mouthed as much of her tremendous right breast as I could and pulled on that. I choked on her fleshy, fiery tit, scouring the firm underside of it with my whipping tongue, before eventually disgorging its dripping, snowy white mass and attacking the girl's other magnificent boob. Then I pushed her globes together and flailed my tongue back and forth across both of their stiffened peaks at once.

"Make love to my pussy!" Daria hissed. "Make me come as I've always fantasized about you making me come!"

As I'd always fantasized about making the succulent siren come! I fell to my knees in the loamy soil and grasped her trembling butt cheeks, staring at the girl's furry sex in dizzy-headed awe for a moment, breathing deeply of the musky scent of her dripping want. She desperately reached down and pulled her pussy lips apart, blinding me with her pink. I swallowed hard and held my breath and plunged my tongue into her slit.

"Yes!" she screamed, clutching her mammoth breasts and savagely kneading them, twisting and pulling on her rosy nipples in a frenzy.

My head spun and my body surged with the intoxicating smell and tangy taste of her pussy, as I resolutely licked her, dragging my beaded tongue over her sticky sex from bumhole to clitty, over and over, lapping at her pussy with an earnestness I was sure would be rewarded and reciprocated. I formed my thick tongue into a hardened blade and drove it deep into my girl's cunt.

"I'm coming!" Daria squealed. Her sweat-sheened, flame-licked body quivered out of control, giant breasts jouncing up and down in her hands and juicy pussy gushing gratitude as she was rocked repeatedly by orgasm while I vigorously fucked her with my tongue.

And when the lovely girl with the lust-inducing body at last calmed down again, I withdrew my tongue from her snatch, licked my slimy lips, and swallowed the remainder of her juices. Then I climbed to my feet, unbuttoned my dress, and let it slide off. I stripped off my undergarments, my heated body gleaming naked and needy in the moonlight, the cool evening air doing nothing to stanch the fire inside. "Care for a piece of my birthday cake, Daria?" I quipped, smiling shakily at the Rubenesque beauty.

Her misty eyes wandered down from my reddened face to my girlish small breasts and woman-hard, cherry-red nipples, then further down my belly till they settled in between my trembling legs. She stared at my pussy, licked her fingers, reached forward, and pressed them against my yearning sex. I groaned with joy. Daria fingered my tingling pussy, turning my legs to jelly and my sex to tears.

Then the delightful girl glanced over my quaking shoulders, and her eyes suddenly flooded with terror rather than nervousness. She pulled her digits away and screamed, "Ohmigod! Run, Velda, run!" She twirled around and fled into the bushes, leaving her clothes and my unconsummated lust behind.

I stood there, confused and frustrated. Then I heard a soft, rustling sound behind me, like that of a bat landing and folding its wings. I spun around—and beheld an exquisite beauty whom I instinctively knew was the Countess Sabrina Comaneci, the evil, erotic, blood-and-soul-sucker my mother had warned me about.

She was small in stature, vertically, but so much, much larger horizontally, where it counted in my book, and she was completely and utterly naked save for a black satin cape with blood-red lining that hung about her shoulders, tied at the neck. Her breasts were absolutely gargantuan, translucent, blue-veined spheres that hung heavily from her chest like overgrown, ivory melons. Her face was a picture-perfect, porcelain oval, hair long and black, and both her face and her hair shone in the light shed by the crackling fire, by the giant, glowing celestial orb in the sky known as Venus.

The Countess spread her arms, her cape, and hissed at me, baring a pair of long, lethal-looking fangs. "I have followed the scent of your need!" she trilled in a voice as sweet as the honeysuckle and deep as the grave, black eyes glittering as they consumed my pussy. "You will satisfy me tonight, as I satisfy you for all time!"

I looked where she was looking, and was astonished to see and feel my continuing wetness. The wicked woman's uninhibited, almost tangible, lust engulfed my ready and willing mind and body, and I felt compelled by some unknown, primal force to reach down and flutter my fingers over the object of her desire and stroke my pussy, fanning the flames of our mutual desire.

The countess shrieked with delight, teeth flashing dazzlingly white. She grabbed up her massive breasts and roughly fondled them, her demon eyes searing my sopping sex. And then, before I could even react, she swooped down upon me, pushing me to the ground with the strength of ten women and mounting my head, shoving her pussy into my face. She let out a scream that shattered the night for miles around, pumping her hips, urgently rubbing her musty, dripping pussy against my lips and nose, grinding it into my open mouth. She roughly pulled on her spike-like nipples and rocked back and forth on my face, moaning as animals moan.

The unearthly eroticism of that sexy she-beast rendered my mind incapable of thought, my muscles incapable of action. Only my tongue gave voice to my towering lust, as I penetrated the countess's slickened, blood-red lips with it.

"Beelzebub, yes!" she cried, frantically gyrating her pussy on my upthrust and extended pink stake. She shoved up her breasts and bit into her impossibly erect nipples, sealing her lips around first one punctured protuberance and then the other, sucking long and hard and deeply.

She endlessly churned her deathly chilled yet sublimely wet pussy back and forth across my lips and tongue, going faster and faster, frenziedly riding my face, building and building her centuries-old passion to what surely had to be a cataclysmic conclusion. And indeed, her pale twin globes suddenly shimmied and her jutting nubs spouted curdled milk and her tombstone-white body rippled as she was jolted repeatedly by brutal orgasm. The satanic siren gushed goo out of her crimson gash, slathering my face and flooding my throat with her furious joy. I could only lie there, dreamy-eyed and defenseless, and take it, unwilling and unable to stop the hellish carnality.

The countess tilted her ecstatic face up to the heavens and howled at the planet Venus, her pussy drowning and suffocating me, before she finally, finally collapsed down onto the ground next to me, panting like a satiated beast. The earth literally had moved, getting ready to swallow me up.

The sexy vampiress then leaned over and licked her mildewy ecstasy off my face in long, slow, satisfied strokes before snaking her tongue into my mouth and down my throat, almost choking me with her gratitude. She gorged herself on my mouth, with her facial lips this time, kissing and frenching me, licking my lips. Then she set her sights a little lower, slithering down my body to get face-to-fur with my smoldering pussy. She spread my molten lips with her talons and began licking my slit with a forked, velvet-sandpaper tongue.

"Jesus!" I groaned ironically, my body weak with her witchery, my pussy ablaze. I'd never had a girl pet my pussy with her tongue before, and the dizzying, deep-body sensation was both out-of-this-world and otherworldly.

The countess stared up at me as I stared down at her, her onyx eyes glittering, depthless pools reflecting my own uncontrollable desire. She pulled me further apart, her thumb buffing my puffed-up clitty now, her nose slick with my juices. She licked and licked my pink, sucked on my clitty, then glided her tongue inside me, probing for my sexual core.

"Mmmm!" I moaned, the wicked lady of the evening's tongue plugging into me and charging my body with sexual energy.

Cool, damp breath steamed out of her flared nostrils and onto my burning cunt, as she fed her tongue into my being. The tip of her tongue bumped up against the thin, fragile barrier that marked my virginity. The Countess grinned evilly at me, her tongue pushing relentlessly forward, her razor-sharp fangs gleaming, growing . . .

◆

MY ECSTASY KNEW NO BOUNDS after the sharp, sweet pain of the initial bloodletting. My dark mistress licked and sucked and bit and drank from my engorged sex as I plaintively and pliantly pushed my hips off the ground to feed her eternal hunger. Soul-shattering ecstasy came quickly and often, till finally, with the harsh, clear light of dawn breaking across the countryside, we were sent scuttling for shelter. Down into a dark, dusty, centuries-old crypt we journeyed, home of the busty Countess Sabrina Comaneci and her many female followers; my home.

ROOM 545

GENEVA NIXON

THE DAY BEGAN just like any other day at the Drake Hotel: boring and dull. My shift usually started around ten a.m., but I arrived a little bit after eleven. I was getting to the point of being sick and tired of cleaning up after people: rock stars who hung bras from chandeliers, drug dealers who spilled heroin in the sink, bachelor parties that ended up with semen stains on the floor. It was enough to make me ill when I thought about it. But it was the Drake, one of the most luxurious hotels of Chicago: definitely not a Super 8. The furniture in the lobby alone was worth more than my entire apartment. And I had moved mountains to make sure I got the damn job in the first place—yet why, I don't remember. All I could think of at the moment was running into the uniform room, punching in, and grabbing my attire. Quickly I changed out of the jeans and shirt I sported and into the white and black cropped skirt, solid white blouse, and name tag. Sometimes we were required to wear the stupid hat, too, but today I wasn't in the mood. Besides, I had just gotten my hair layered and relaxed the previous day: I wasn't about to let some hat hide my sexy do.

Slipping past the manager, Richard, who patrolled the lobby waiting to home in on me about being late, I crept into the service closet and picked out a buggy to use. Making sure Richard was still looking for me in the lobby, which was crowded with people checking in and out, I made my way to the elevators and then on up to the eleventh floor.

"Housekeeping," I said while knocking on the first door. I'd usually say this twice, knock three times, and if there was no answer, I'd open the door with a service key. Unfortunately someone answered.

"You know what time it is," came the voice on the other side of the door. It had to be a guy in his mid-forties who was busy playing with his erect soldier. His voice sounded a little exasperated and embarrassed—a major giveaway. I smiled to myself, wondering if he wasn't getting any at home.

"Go away. I don't need housekeeping right now," he blurted out. All I could do was flip him off without his knowing and say, "I apologize, sir."

I moved on down the hall to the next door number on my list, 543. This time some young girl, probably twelve, opened the door.

"Yeah?" she said. She stood there holding the door, looking at me as if I were someone totally beneath her. It was obvious she was from Connecticut; she carried that pompous attitude, the one you develop when your father is part of the Yachting Club and your mother downs martinis more frequently than water. I looked her up and down, wondering if she'd ever grow out of this awkward phase.

"Housekeeping, miss. Would you like me to come in?"

"Uh, I'm on the phone right now so I would appreciate it if you came back *later*," and with that she shut the door in my face.

I had to stand there for a moment to regain my composure. I've had doors closed in my face many times, but never from some Paris Hilton pubescent bitch. But after a minute or two I nodded my head, sighed, and moved on to the next door. After all, it was part of the job.

Room 545. I stared at the numbers on the door, loving the way the hump of the five was shaped. I've always admired the strangest things. I snapped out of it soon enough and began the routine of knocking, calling, knocking.

"Housekeeping." No answer. I knocked again.

"Housekeeping," I repeated, this time a little louder than before. Still no answer.

I grabbed the key with relief and slid it into the slot. The light flashed green and I opened the door. The room was more or less the same as the others on the floor, except that it carried one large king-size bed with an adjoining suite area. This usually included a red roped couch with feathered pillows, two matching wingback chairs, and an amber marble coffee table. Obviously it was one of the more expensive rooms; most of the lighting was track. And there was a desk in the corner, along with a smaller chair that was used frequently by the wealthy traveling-businessman type. However, the first thing that caught my attention was not really the lighting or the pricey armoire—it was the woman who was completely naked pleasing herself in the bed.

I stood around the hallway corner gawking at what she was doing. She had her eyes firmly closed, so I knew she couldn't see me. She was also moaning now and then into a pillow that was gripped by her left hand, so that must've been the reason she didn't hear me either. From head to toe she was covered in little beads of sweat. Trickles of them would slide off her stomach to the left and to the right. Her breast carried them as if passengers on a boat, holding dearly to the anchor of her nipples. She breathed in and out so deeply that I thought she was hyperventilating, but it seemed this was just her way of enjoying the moment. Her right hand lay over the completely bare pussy between her legs, slowly rubbing her clit in motions that my eyes couldn't help but follow. She would curl her toes once in a while, experiencing the moment of delight, letting it glide over her in a ripple that shook her entire frame. Strands of her hair, which was a murky brown, stuck to her forehead and to her face. Sometimes she would let the pillow go, brushing her hair off her, only to have it return when she'd jerk her head. The tongue in my mouth wanted desperately to drink her perspiration, for it seemed like an oasis in the middle of a sweltering desert or rain that came from her pores, giving life to the hair follicles all over her body. I marveled at the sheen it gave to her skin—skin the color of buttermilk itself.

It was obvious she was relentless in her pursuit of pleasure. Her fingers had slipped inside of her on more than one occasion. My own breathing began to increase when I saw this happen, and I too moved my right hand closer to the wanting between my legs. It was easy for me to get past the garments I wore; the skirt was short enough to pull up at the hem. Sliding my fingers under my panties, which were saturated from watching her, I stuck my own fingers inside of me. I had to lean against the wall, pushing my left hand against it to keep myself up. Quietly opening my legs wider, pushing my fingers deeper inside of myself, I watched while she did the same. I could feel the lining of my pussy pulse with blood and sweet wetness, and every time I looked at her fingers enter and exit her, my pulse would quicken. A flow of moisture escaped from me and fled down my inner thigh. I felt it hit every hair on its way, giving my body goose bumps all over. I swooned at this, closing my eyes and enjoying its trek. I dug my fingers deeper inside of me, getting to the root of the pulse itself. My nails scratched me inside, causing little gasps from my mouth, but I didn't care. I stayed where I was, leaning against the wall with my arm as a prop, letting wetness spill from me down my leg, closing my eyes in all of it with deep enjoyment.

It was then that I opened my eyes in the moment of release and saw the woman staring right back at me.

A deer caught in headlights, I dared not move. I must've been too loud because she wasn't just looking at me, she was standing practically in front of me: I hadn't heard her move at all.

"You came?" she asked, looking me up and down, noticing the trail of wetness along my thigh.

I wanted to answer her, but my mouth was frozen. I honestly didn't know what to do. So I just stood there, my fingers still inside of me, listening to her breathe.

"If you did, I'm glad you enjoyed the show." She said this with a half grin, flashing her ivory teeth behind her pink lips. She stepped closer to me, looking at me again up and down. I didn't step back.

"I'm sorry," I said, as if I had done something terribly wrong. As if I were some schoolgirl who'd just cheated on a test and gotten caught. The words were a surprise to me because I really wasn't sorry at all.

"It's okay. I wanted you to come in. I heard you when you called." Once again she gave me the grin. I was stunned when she told me this; she had actually *planned* on my seeing her. However, at the same time I was a little excited by it. It had been a long time since a woman had captured my interest so quickly. She must be something to reckon with, I mused.

She then grabbed my hand, sliding my fingers out of me, and placed every last digit in her mouth, one by one. My jaw dropped a bit, not knowing if I should turn around and leave or let her continue to suck the come off. Whatever the case, it was quite arousing, and I'm sure she could sense this. Her teeth grazed the tips of my fingers before they exited her warm mouth. When I looked at them, there were little imprints of where she had bitten them, causing me to be all the more aroused. She lifted her own fingers, the very same ones she had just used a moment earlier, and delicately touched my lips. My tongue slowly slid out of my mouth across them, immediately tasting her. There was a zing that ran throughout my body when my tongue hit her index finger, one that tripled my arousal. I was at the brim of the cup by now; pretty soon I would overflow.

She stepped even closer to me and kissed me softly. Her mouth was unbelievably hot against my own. I had no choice but to grab her and force her even closer to me. Her body was still covered in beads of sweat; she wore them as if they were a bodily decoration. My hands slid across them, gathering them into small pools beneath my palms. Her body wasn't hesitant in the face of my presumption in the slightest. She fell right into my arms as if she had been waiting for this all along. My mouth clamped over hers harder, pulling her tongue into me. She pushed her way inside of my mouth, greedily taking my kisses with such fever.

Pretty soon I was leaning my back against the wall, holding her in front of me. Her knee had found its way between my legs and was nudging at the moisture that was accumulating there. Moans escaped our mouths, finding shelter in the other's, as we kissed each other passionately. She stopped for a moment and looked me in the eyes, searching for recognition of want and desire. I stared back at her, trying with all my might not to grind against her knee that was pushing at my clit, helplessly captivated by her gaze. I would've done anything for her at the moment; I was that hypnotized.

She smiled and kissed me again, this time a little softer than before. I still held her, not daring to let her go. Her breasts heaved against my blouse, piercing me with their nipples. I could tell there was something she wanted.

"What?" I asked, breaking the silence of passion.

"I was just wondering if your clit tastes as good as your fingers."

I had to restrain myself from laughing; people just didn't talk like this in the real world. But I did grin at her. So she wanted to eat me out, huh? Well, I could definitely go for that.

"Why don't you get down there and find out," I said in a demanding tone of voice. Now it was her turn to be stunned. I'm sure she didn't think I could be so vigorous, but if we were going to play this game, then it was time to put on the poker face.

She happily kneeled before me, lifting up my skirt, looking up at me as well. I looked down at her, placing my hands on her shoulders, rubbing them gently. She slid down my panties, taking them off me one leg at a time, kissing my knees afterwards. Her hands began to caress my inner thighs, spreading them apart at the same time, opening me to the point that I felt a breeze. My clit was throbbing—more like pounding, begging for attention. I was afraid that it was the size of an acorn; it felt that engorged. But as soon as I thought this, her mouth engulfed it, causing me to arch my waist into her face, tilting my upper back against the wall. My fingers ran over her shoulders, squeezing them as she sucked on me, letting my eyes roll in delight while my head fell backwards. Her mouth was still unbelievably hot, and now that it was pressed against my secluded pearl, it was even hotter. I moaned and moaned, now placing my fingers in her hair, pressing her mouth closer to me as my waist bobbed back and forth, keeping her in place. She sucked and sucked so hard, enjoying it more than I. I could feel my orgasm build from the tips of my toes on up. I clutched my hands tighter to her head, moving faster in my thrusting.

She must've known that I was about to come because she ripped her mouth away from me. For a split second I felt amazingly naked down there, with no warmth of anything to cover me. She grabbed my hand and led me to the bed in a frenzy, pushing me down face first. I landed with a *thud*, wondering if she was going to spank me or something. She then lay down beside me, situating herself on her back.

"Put it over my face . . . now."

I did nothing but comply. In a matter of seconds I had my pussy right over her mouth, practically sitting on her face, but distributing my weight evenly to my bent legs. I couldn't see her face because my skirt was covering it, but I could feel exactly what she was doing. Her tongue had worked its way straight up inside of me, licking the lining of my inner walls, whipping over and over against them. I leaned forward, pressing the palms of my hands to the mattress, grinding my pussy onto this lovely stake. Up and down I pounced as she wrapped her arms around my thighs, bringing me down when I'd go up. The faster I moved the faster she'd drill me with her tongue, lashing it relentlessly in the depths of me. I knew I was flowing into her mouth; I could feel it when she'd stop and drink from me. This thought ravaged my brain, making me all the more wet for her. I knew I was about to come.

"I'm coming . . . I'm coming," I cried out, bouncing up and down on her with such speed and execution. She lapped at me harder, digging her nails into my thighs. I released powerfully into her mouth, feeling myself burst like a fire hydrant on a hot summer day in the Bronx. She drank all of me then, reveling in it. I fell forward as soon as I was done, breathing ten times harder than my normal rate. She moved out from under me, licking her lips. I lay down on my stomach with my head to the side, looking at her. She acted like she'd just tasted the fruit of the gods. She leaned on her elbow on her side facing me, running her fingers over my bare ass. By now I had caught my breath. I just lay there, though, looking at her, wondering what she tasted like herself.

"You could find out," she said. She smiled, knowing that she had just read my mind.

I pushed myself up off the bed, standing at the foot of it. She had turned over now onto her back, leaning on her elbows. I grabbed her legs and dragged her wonderfully naked body to the edge of the bed, propping her heels up at the end. Spreading her I saw what she truly was: bare and succulently juicy. I looked up at her and she smiled, still remaining on her elbows. I got down on my knees in front of her, diving right in with my mouth. The taste of her burst like a thousand Black Cats in my mouth. Her pussy was incredibly wet, with juice dripping right out of her onto my tongue. I lapped at her from side to side, feeling the pulsating lining of her walls. Every so often they would squeeze against me, trying to barricade me. But I was far too persistent in my work. I grabbed her legs and opened her lower mouth wider, pushing my tongue deeper into her, hitting the tip of her cervix, climbing higher then she could believe. She tossed her head left to right, moaning louder with every passing second. Her hands gripped the covers of the bed, only to let them go, as she would then grip her own breasts. She repeated this while I glanced up occasionally; her body was totally surrendering to me. She'd beg me for more with her moans, asking me to eat her pussy. Oh, I was enjoying myself more than I could imagine, feasting on her while she didn't fight it.

Her hips rocked up and down off the bed, her heels digging into the edge. Trails of wetness slid down out of her. I licked them up individually, placing my tongue back in her afterwards. She clenched at me, pulling me in with her own inner muscles. I submitted myself to this; deeper I pushed into her, closer I moved my mouth to her, tasting and smelling her true womanhood. My hands ran up and down her thighs, squeezing them and pinching them. Her moaning would hit a higher note every time I did this, telling me that she loved it.

"I'm going to come," she screamed, grabbing her hair and arching her back. Her spurt hit me hard in the throat, giving me shivers from head to toe. Her own body shivered as she came, clenching the covers tightly as she moaned for me with orgasmic relief. I blew inside of her and then sucked out; I wanted every morsel of her in me. Her savor was fantastic, so beyond what I thought it would be.

She withdrew from the edge of the bed, moving more to the center. I clambered back on, lying next to her. She rolled over to me on her side and exhaled deeply.

"You're something else."

I couldn't help but smile, always smiling, but it was all that I could do. She was a type of woman that I'd never met before: a pure beast. I reveled in it. There was nothing in the world I enjoyed more than an insatiable appetite for sex. She sat up and flipped her hair off her shoulder. She made her way off the bed and over to the desk. She reached into one of the drawers. What she drew out practically made me pant like a bitch in heat.

"Before you leave, I'm gonna fuck you with this strap-on, so that when you do leave, you'll be able to still feel me inside of you . . . all day long."

I nodded obediently, getting off the bed, walking over to her. She slipped it on, one leg at a time, pulling it right over her drenched pussy. The size had to be around 8 inches: mammoth in comparison to mine at home. I moved in closer to her, going to touch it, for I just wanted to feel its hardness in my hand, but while I extended my arm to cop a feel, she pulled me against the desk, bending me over it. She stood behind me now, kicking my legs apart. She slid all 8 inches of that rubber cock inside of my pussy. I nearly screamed, for I was tighter than I thought. But soon her thrusting became a rhythm I picked up on. Back and forth we moved as one, slowly. She knew I needed to get used to it before she rammed me the way she wanted.

"It's okay, baby, just take it slow right now," she said, rubbing her hands against the back of my blouse. I unbuttoned it and took it off, surprised that I hadn't already. She kissed my back then, showing gratitude. Her fingers slid across my skin, unclasping my bra, cupping my breasts as they swayed with our motion. Soon my pussy began to loosen, getting used to the feel of her strap. I was grateful for this; I wanted desperately for her to fuck me madly.

Lifting my skirt a little higher, she thrust against me hard. By now the desk was rocking itself, making small creaks. My flailing arms had moved every piece of paper on it to the floor, nearly knocking over the computer itself. She began to fuck me faster, letting her thrusts show her eagerness. I felt my whole body cave against the desk each time she lunged.

"Ask me to fuck you," she commanded in between her pushes. Over and over she hammered against my ass, driving her strap right against my G-spot.

"Please . . . fuck me," I moaned out, letting her movements take over me. I was beyond all types of saturation; my pussy was nothing but an ocean now. My chest heaved with her every shove against the wood. Louder the desk began to creak, but not louder than my moaning.

"Harder?" she asked, slapping my ass at the very same time.

A surge of shock ran up my spine when she did this, making me bite my lip with delicious pain. "Harder," I screamed, pushing my open pussy back onto her strap. I wanted more, so much more.

She fucked me faster now, not letting even seconds pass between her thrusts. My body ached from slamming into the wood, the edge of it hitting me in the gut. But I didn't care; I wanted this so badly. My whole body needed to be obliterated by this woman, whoever she was.

She slapped me again, this time directly on the left cheek. I could feel the warmth of the handprint she no doubt left there. I moaned for her this time, letting her know I was pleased when she hit me. Pushing my ass right against her stomach as her strap overwhelmed my cunt, I could feel myself begin to tighten. This one was going to be big.

"I'm gonna come," I shouted, breathing harder with every lunge she gave me. Letting my moans carry to the ceiling and back down to my ears.

She pulled my hair then, forcing my neck back, fucking me faster than before, using her other hand to pinch my nipple.

"Then come to me."

And with that I let go of one of the biggest orgasms I have ever had. I laid the top half of my body flat against the desk, clawing my nails at the wood. My lower half almost jumped off the floor, remaining on tiptoes while I came. Rushes of warmth ran throughout me directly to the tip of her strap. My voice gave out; all that was left was movement and hard breathing. She lay against my back when I was done, kissing my skin. Sweat had pooled there, but she didn't mind, she kissed anyway, licking a bit as well.

We stayed in that position for a while, me catching my breath, her listening to it through my back. She still remained inside of me, and I didn't mind. I wasn't ready for her to part just yet. I closed my eyes and enjoyed the moment. Never have I been so humbled while still being so superior. This mystery woman had just beaten me and let me win. I was standing perfectly on the line between sex and pure lust.

Eventually she rose up off me, pulling out as well. I pulled myself up off the desk and turned around to look at her. Her strap was covered with me. She was marvelously beautiful to me then, more stunning then when I first set eyes on her. And we both knew that we had gotten to the core of the other, reaching a place where each wished to live. She leaned over and kissed my cheek then, patting the other side with her hand.

"Thank you," she said, so simply that I couldn't give a reply. Whatever she had really needed for me to say or do, I had already done.

She left me standing there, watching her as she took off her erection and walked into the bathroom. The door was closed then, but I could hear the bathwater begin to run. I turned and grabbed my bra, snapping it back in place, putting my blouse back over it. While heading for the door I took a look at myself in the hall mirror. My face was flushed but I was radiant. I laughed at myself, at how something so out of the norm had changed my entire demeanor. I spruced up my hair a bit, working it back into its original do, put my panties back on, and turned to leave.

As I closed the door behind me I took another look at the numbers on the door. I smiled while checking out the shape of the five. I had always admired the strangest things.

ROOM WITH A VIEW

KIMBERLY LAFONTAINE

MY BABY KNOWS HOW to fuck me. She knows how to make me squirm and writhe and beg for it. She knows when my clit is just hard enough that one more flick with her tongue will send me over the edge.

She knows that when she wakes up in the middle of the night, all she has to do is snuggle up to my back and grind her hips against my ass to make my pussy soaking wet and that she can reach between my legs from behind and fuck me within seconds.

Sometimes, I wake up in the middle of the night with her already inside, pounding me. I wake up with a moan on my lips that quickly turns to sharp breaths and screams. And she'll bring me hard and fast—a minute, maybe two or three—her groans in my ears, my right arm reaching back to hold as much of her as I can reach. She'll pull out, circle my clit, run that wetness all over me, and slide right back in for more.

Occasionally, she'll rub my come on my tits. Sometimes, she'll lick it off her fingers with her eyes closed, savoring the taste. And most often, she'll let me flip over and get to work on her.

Oh, yeah, she knows how to work me over.

It's that wild, clawing, can't get enough, desperately hungry for each other kind of sex. The type where you get slammed up against a wall with your face pressed in the plaster, your knees weak, barely able to draw enough breath between animalistic screams. The type of fucking where you walk in the door and get grabbed by your jacket collar and yanked in for a forceful, deliciously rough kiss that melts you from the inside out.

I'd never had a lover who got me the way she did; such a confident, strong woman, so sure she'd get what she wanted if she pushed me just the right way.

I'd always been the driver, the dominant, the top—whatever you want to call it. You'd never have found me on all fours, my ass in the air, submissive as submissive could be. That was until she came along.

Let's call my sexy honey Britt.

Britt is no butch. And certainly no femme. She can be as girly as any femme—worried about which shirt goes best with which linen capris (and damn, she knows how to dress well). But she can also be as macho as any hard-core dyke—talking about her cock and how she's gonna fuck me in the ass with it someday, how she's got a hard-on with my name on it, and how she's gonna tear into me.

It's hard to put her in any category, not that it's necessary to classify anybody. Especially if they're just really fucking sexy and it doesn't matter in what way.

Damn, she's hot with her peppered, cropped hair that makes her look like a lesbian version of George Clooney, her pale, piercing blue eyes and athletic build, runner's legs, strong arms and hands—beautiful—with a soft back, tattoos, sexy breasts, and a nice ass that I want to grope as often as possible.

Her lips are soft and we kiss well—sometimes tender and loving, sometimes fierce and wild. She's the most physical, passionate lover I've ever had. And she can go from beautiful romance to fuck-me-now slut faster than I thought possible. Gotta love a versatile woman.

It's like being at a feast with all your favorite dishes and some you didn't even know you'd like but discover you love.

I'd known that she could take me places I'd never been and had longed for so desperately. She'd already proven that many times in the very short time that we'd crossed the line from friends to lovers.

But I hadn't known that she would be the woman who'd take my fantasy and do her damned best to make it true. She was on a mission and all I had to do was ask or suggest. It took a trip out of state to a writer's conference and some offhand comments to make me realize she was that kind of lover.

Maybe we weren't serious. Maybe I wanted to be. And maybe we both had too many damned hang-ups at the time—recent heartbreak on both sides and tons of regret. If we handled our emotional shit as well as we handled making love, we'd be champs in the relationship department. But for that weekend, I was not about to let the drama of our whirlwind romance spoil the mood. Screw age differences and consequences and baggage.

I'd pretend we were perfectly happy. In love. Together the way I wanted. That she was mine and I was hers and there was nobody else. She'd wanted to be there for me, to support my writing. It was sweet in a way that meant so much to me and I couldn't help but feel that the trip would bring us closer, both in friendship and in love.

And yes, I knew she loved me, too. That much was obvious. Britt could deny with her words but couldn't lie with her watery blue eyes.

So if we had a hell of a lot of sex while we were there, all the better. Because I don't sleep around. Meaningless fucking isn't my cup of tea.

She'd rented us a suite. A nice one. It was nearly at the top of the high-rise hotel where the conference was being held. The "sweet suite," as I called it, had a ceiling-to-floor window that encompassed an entire wall. The view was spectacular—all city lights and skyscrapers opposite. I'd only been able to admire the view after we'd stumbled into the hotel room, ripped off our clothes, and fucked for an hour.

When I did mention it, I added half-hopefully and more than a touch nervous for bringing up what she didn't know was a longstanding fantasy, "I'd love it if you fucked me against that window. That would be hot."

More bravely than I felt, I climbed out of bed and walked over to said window, pressed my face and hands against it, moving my hips just enough to get her attention. I was a little anxious being this close to the only thing that kept me from falling to my death, that thin piece of glass.

I have a fear of heights. Twenty floors up is scary as hell. She didn't know that, either. Sex with a little fear, I thought, and felt my clit throb. "Would you do that for me?"

"Really?" she murmured, wrapping her arms around my waist and grinding into me so that my breasts pressed into the glass. "You'd like that, huh?" God, her voice is so fucking sexy, low and sultry. "Is that a fantasy of yours?"

I nodded, trembling.

"Then we just might have to do something about that." A pause. "I want to make all your fantasies come true."

"Mmm" was all I could manage with her body pressed so distractingly close to mine and my throat tight. I ordered my mind to shut down and not think about the fantasies involving a beach and a ceremony to surface.

"Fuck," she murmured and laughed, then pulled back reluctantly, slapping my ass. "Definitely. But we have to go."

Damn conference, I thought, and turned to face her with a resigned but anticipatory smile on my lips. "Yeah, we have to go. We're already going to be a little late."

She cupped my face and touched her forehead to mine. "Tonight," was all she said. But that one word made my insides tighten almost painfully, chasing away the emotional turmoil, fixating on the fact that I could barely believe she was talking about doing it for real.

Not just maybe. Tonight.

There was a social dinner for the company's staff that I had to attend. Britt was my guest. I'd been looking forward to this dinner for a long time. My co-workers/friends and I didn't get to see one another often as most business was conducted online and we were scattered all across the country. But I also couldn't get "Tonight" out of my head. That she kept touching and squeezing my thigh under the table at dinner didn't help. That I'd come down to dinner freshly fucked and seriously turned on didn't help, either. My clit was hard. I was sure my thong was soaked.

Through the restaurant windows, I saw the darkness grow outside. If we left the lights on in the room, I thought dreamily, people in the high-rise opposite ours might be able to see us fucking. The newly discovered exhibitionist in me purred in anticipation. I began to seriously ache for need of being filled up.

The discussions around me began to blur into meaningless chatter after the first hour. I didn't know how much more I could take. If she slid her hand up between my legs to tease me one more time, I knew I was going to let a moan slip; then there'd be more than the light teasing to endure from my coworkers, who were already making crass comments about the way Britt and I looked at each other.

She leaned into me and whispered in my ear, "Time to go yet?"

I scanned the length of the table, took in the half-empty plates and women eating. "Not yet." She groaned, and I couldn't help but empathize.

Finally, another hour later, the plates were empty and conversation began to wane. It was now or never. I stood up, thanked my boss heartily for dinner, took Britt's hand, and led her away. So we were the first ones to leave. To hell with it. I don't think a single one of those women didn't expect it anyway.

We said little as we walked as quickly as we could without running. The hallways from the hotel restaurant to the lobby seemed endless. At last, Britt punched the elevator button hard. And again. And again. The bell chimed, the doors opened, and we slipped inside. She jabbed the button to close the doors. Then she shoved me against the wall and pinched my nipples, kissing me furiously before breaking apart when the elevator slowed and reached our floor. We exited, both gasping.

My heart was pounding, my knees felt weak. My whole body was tingling and flushed. Fuck, I was wet. I could feel how slippery my thong was, rubbing against me as we practically ran hand in hand down the hall toward our room. She fumbled with the card, got the damned door open, and hit the lights. The door hadn't even fallen shut yet before we were in each other's arms, tearing at shirts and pants, ripping them off and tossing them on the floor.

Britt groaned, cursed, and bit my arm so hard I knew it was going to bruise. The pain only fueled my furious desire to come against the window. I tried to edge toward it, but she gripped me hard by the waist and spun me around, bending me over the floorboard of the bed. She grabbed the back of my neck and pushed my head down low, trailing the fingers of her free hand through my swollen lips. I spread my legs eagerly for her, just like I always did—with a sigh and a whimper.

When she realized just how wet I was, she moaned long and low, "Like butter," then thrust three fingers inside in one smooth move. She tore a surprised scream from my throat.

"Fuck, you're nasty."

"You love it," I gasped, trembling. I'd been needing her all night and within moments was close. So close.

"Not yet," she growled and withdrew, letting go of my neck and spinning me around.

I cupped her face with both hands and dove in for a series of searing kisses, my hands slowly crawling up and around the back of her head, grabbing her hair, pulling her in, crushing our lips together.

"Wrap your legs around me," she demanded when we broke apart for air. I obeyed immediately. At that point, I'd have done anything she asked so long as the promise of her fingers inside me was still in the game.

She cupped my ass, lifted, and marched us over to the window. I felt the cool pane press against my back as she ground herself against me, her hands kneading my breasts—rolling my nipples between thumbs and forefingers, pulling and twisting my nipple ring sharply.

"Please," I begged shamelessly.

"Please what?"

"Fuck me, Britt. Please fuck me. I need you. I need you now."

She released my breasts and wedged a hand between our bodies. I clawed at her back, already damp with a light sheen of sweat. When she penetrated me, I groaned a guttural version of her name. She pulled back agonizingly slow before thrusting herself in me again hard, forcing another cry and groan from my lips.

"Yeah?" she asked, and I opened my clenched eyes. A knowing, smug, sexy smile was playing on her lips.

"Yeah," I sighed, rotating my hips to meet her thrust.

"Is this what you wanted?" She added a fourth finger and thrust inside me again.

My head was drooping forward, our foreheads touching as we stared into each other's eyes, our gasping breaths mingling.

"Yes," I hissed, digging my fingers and heels into her back, squeezing her waist with my thighs, my whole body trying to suck her in. "Damn, you fuck me so well."

At this, her resolve seemed to crumble and she moaned, rapidly picking up speed—her fingers sliding in and out, her thumb rubbing my clit in time with every pounding thrust, harder and harder until my whole body was sliding up and down the glass.

She grunted and groaned. I wanted to hang on, wanted to make it last, but her words, “I’m going to come, I’m going to come, I’m going to come inside you,” made me convulse around her instantly, screaming her name.

Britt’s eyes slid shut and a shudder ran the length of her spine. I could almost feel her coming in me as her movements slowed—still sliding in and out, but tenderly now—until she finally pulled out and circled my clit, her head lolling onto my chest, her breathing ragged. Sweat trickled from her forehead down my stomach.

I rested my head against the glass, panting, and unwrapped my legs from her waist, sliding down the window and discovering that I could barely stand.

Less than a minute passed before our lips met again. But she tore away from the kiss abruptly and spun me roughly. “Hands on the glass,” she growled, grabbed one breast from behind, and slid back inside.

“Fuck,” I hissed, surprised, but the sensation of being filled again when I’d just gone tight from orgasm wasn’t unwelcome.

And then I saw what I suspected she wanted me to see—that sparkling city view.

My hands and forehead and tits pressed against the glass, my legs spread for my lover with her fingers buried deep in my pussy, I realized that lights were on in some of the rooms in the hotel opposite ours.

Figures were moving around near the windows. Surely we

could be seen. I wondered what they'd think of our fucking. Would they turn away or would they stand transfixed by the sight? Could they see us as clearly as I could see them? Surely.

"Oh, Britt, Britt, Britt . . ." The words tumbled from my mouth, hot breath fogging the windows. "That's good. That's so fucking good."

I came again. Harder than the first time. She didn't stop pounding me. I came again. And again. And again until she shuddered and slowed.

"Baby?" she whispered after a few moments had passed in silence save for the gasp when she withdrew and our heavy breathing.

"Yeah?"

"Give me some head?"

"Mmm," I chuckled. "Yeah, I'll suck your clit, baby. I'll suck it down my throat all night long after what you just did. Tonight you can have whatever the hell you want."

"Just tonight?"

"Any night."

After I gave her head, we fucked again. This time between the sheets. She made her requests—"Straddle me" and "I want you with your ass in the air" and "I want your come all over my face" —until we were both so exhausted we fell asleep, our bodies wrapped together tightly.

After that incredible Friday night, I never had any qualms about sharing ideas and fantasies again. I'd tell her what I wanted and we'd try it out, that smug, sexy grin on her face, a look of wonder and delight on mine.

Toys. Airplane sex. Getting fingerfucked on a train full of passengers. Whatever I wanted.

Maybe we'd figure out our emotional mess. Eventually. In the meantime, I knew I'd submit to whatever she wanted sexually. I'd plant seeds and give her ideas, never knowing when she'd come back to fulfill my dreams, but knowing full well that she always would.

Because at the very least, my baby knows how to fuck me. And she does it so well.

SOMETHING I GAVE HER

SANDRA ROTH

I KNEW IT WAS ONE of her choice fantasies: two mean-ass tops screwing one quivering bottom, two butch women nailing one femme, two men fucking one woman—as long as the sexual energy was right, who cared what physical form it took? We'd talked about it in theory; we'd played it out in our heads. She said as long as I was in control, she was up for anything. She especially liked the idea of being asleep or drunk, anything that put her at my mercy. I knew she could take it, too. She was cock-hungry; her ass, her mouth, her pussy, they all ached to be filled, and believe me, her eyes weren't any bigger than her stomach, if you know what I mean, and I think you do.

Last time we were fucking, me whispering how I'd like to line up a team of guys in front of her, make her service them all, she blinked those pretty eyes at me and moaned, "Okay, baby, I'm ready. Anything you want. Anytime, anywhere."

After we finished fucking and she lay there all limp and languid, I said, "Baby, did you mean that? Are you sure?"

"Yes," she said simply. "You set it up, you arrange it."

And just like that she consented. Now here she is, out cold.

See, Tara is a lightweight. She always says she's a cheap date because half a glass of wine makes her tipsy, one mixed drink sends her over the edge. Whenever she says that, I tell her she ain't just a cheap date, she's a cheap whore. That sends her over the edge, too. Tonight she's a goner, just lying there across the bed, her white blouse wrinkled, her button front denim skirt short enough to reveal the tops of her creamy thighs. I see Chris looking at her. She'd like a piece of Tara.

"Sit down, why don't you?" I tell Chris, taking a seat to Tara's right.

Chris looks uncomfortable. She's had too much to drink herself. Hell, maybe I have too, but I'm not feeling it. I'm hot and in control. I knew I could coax enough beer into Chris so she'd have to stay the night, knew a couple of drinks would knock Tara flat. Chris finally plops down on Tara's other side. She leans back against the headboard and rubs her hand across her eyes.

"I should really give Cathy a call," she says, referring to her stubby little girlfriend. Chris could do so much better than Cathy. She's just in a bad way. Her last girlfriend dumped her after ten good years. Chris'd rather bed down with the plain girl she knows won't leave her than take her chances on the open market. But just 'cause she's acting dead doesn't mean she's ready to be buried. I've seen her looking at Tara. I know what she wants. Tonight she's gonna get it.

Soon as that thought crosses my mind, apprehension marches right in after it. Maybe this isn't such a good idea. What if Tara wakes up raw and sore and pissed as hell? Yeah, she consented. However, what if the fantasy turns her on but the reality is just too real?

I shoot a glance at Chris. I know Tara thinks she's hot. Maybe not as built as I am, maybe not as bright, but she's funny and kind and she's got a husky deep voice and the kind of swagger I know knocks Tara out. But shit, Tara *is* knocked out, and who knows if Chris even goes for this kind of kinked-up bullshit.

Chris sits forward to take off her baseball jacket. She rolls up the sleeves of her denim shirt and leans back again. I know exactly where I want this to go; hell, I've only wacked off to it a thousand times, but something stops me from making my move.

"So," Chris interrupts my thoughts, "I gotta tell you, you were right about Tara. She really can't hold her liquor. I mean, look at that." Chris gestures toward Tara's inert form. "Out like a light."

I laugh, "I know, man. And I was hoping for some action tonight."

"Well, hey," says Chris with a shrug, "she's your girlfriend. You're the one who's out there earning the money that keeps her in these cute little outfits. You should get what you pay for."

I know Chris is kidding, I can tell by her sheepish half smile, but her words encourage me.

"I know, right?" I say. "What do I care whether she's conscious or not? Her pussy'll feel the same either way."

"Right, right," Chris starts to respond, but even though she knows about Tara's fantasy, she looks at me, sorta shocked. I told you she was kind.

"I'm just joking." I fold my hands behind my head. I'm not joking, of course, but Chris'll know that soon enough. I'm still uneasy, though, so I take a good hard look at Tara splayed out on the bed. I've seen how she gets around Chris, all giggly, warming to her attention like a high school girl with her favorite teacher. And Chris is all over that shit like white on rice. Okay, it's time to get things rolling.

"So." I turn on my side to face Chris. "How'd you and Cathy meet again?"

As I talk, I trail one hand slowly down Tara's arm. She doesn't move.

"Concert." Chris shrugs. "I was working security, a bunch of people rushed the stage. She got kinda flattened, but I helped her up and we just started talking."

I nod, continue to stroke my hand over Tara's body.

"You two moved in together pretty quick. Seems like you didn't even mention you'd met someone, suddenly you're living together."

"Yeah, well." Chris eyes my hand as it moves over Tara's chest.

"You just couldn't wait, huh?" I pause and finger Tara's nipple. I know Chris can see it harden at my touch. Tara's shirt is so thin; you'd have to be blind to miss it.

"Um," Chris gulps. "Couldn't wait for what?"

"To be together, right? You and Cathy?"

"Naw, we weren't in a rush, just that her lease was up and she was running out of money so . . . I don't know, she just moved in."

I nod, tracing my fingertips over Tara's parted lips. "Well, whatever brought you two together, the important thing is you love her, right? I mean she's good for you and all?"

"Yeah," Chris says quickly. "She's a real sweetheart, wouldn't hurt a fly." Chris stops watching my hand and meets my eye. "I need that right now, you know?" She looks back at my hand.

"Mmm," I say. "Hey, you gotta feel this."

"Feel what?"

"I swear, Tara's got the softest skin in the world. Touch her arm, right here." I indicate the inside of Tara's elbow. Chris looks a little doubtful, but she doesn't hesitate any. She's been waiting to dig her fingers into this soft, cushiony flesh—probably wants to dig something else in even more.

"That *is* soft," she says.

"You think that's soft, feel right here." Again, Chris seems unsure, but that doesn't stop her from stroking her hand over Tara's clavicle, down into the V of her blouse.

"You want another beer?"

"Nah, I'm good." Chris is still running her fingers over Tara's skin.

"So, how come Cathy didn't go tonight?"

"Oh, it's stupid." Chris draws her hand back abruptly. "We had a fight."

"What about?"

"Well, she had to wake up early for her craft show in the morning—you know she makes jewelry and stuff out of safety pins and beads—and she didn't want to stay out late is all."

"So what did you fight about?"

"Oh, nothing really, just, Cathy's a homebody, I guess. When she gets home from work at the end of the day, she just wants to relax."

"There's more than one way to relax."

"That's what I tell her, but you know, people got different sex drives, and it's not like I'm a big partier or anything, but it's Friday night, why not go out, have a couple of drinks, get a little . . . you know . . ."

"I know. So she wanted you to stay home with her?"

"Yeah, and she wasn't feeling too good." Chris lowers her voice. "Female problems, you know?"

Funny how Chris is not a bit ashamed to feel up my unconscious girlfriend just 'cause I tell her to, but she's afraid to say the word "period" out loud. While she's talking, Chris's hand finds its way back to the hollow of Tara's collarbone.

"Anyway, I told her maybe if she came out with us, had a few laughs, loosened up a little, she'd feel better, but she says she doesn't like the way I am around you. Says I get too loud, call too much attention to myself. I told her maybe she could stand to get a little bit loud herself, and she got all mad 'cause she thought I was criticizing her." Chris shakes her head. "Anyway, she decided to stay home and sulk."

Normally I would never say anything like this, but I'm feeling reckless. "Just what you want, right? A sulky bitch with PMS who'd rather make a Christmas ornament then let you fuck her." As soon as I say it Chris's hand stops in mid-stroke. She looks upset. Then she laughs.

"Yeah, just what I want." She keeps laughing, and maybe it's the beer talking, but she says, "No, this here is more like what I want, but then, you knew that." She half-smiles like she's joking, but I know she's serious, and I further know she's scared.

Now, don't get the wrong idea here. If some guy or girl on the street said something like that about Tara, I'd be on him or her in a flash. Nobody makes a pass at what's mine—that is, unless I want them to.

I smile magnanimously at Chris.

"My friend, what's mine is yours."

Chris laughs and her eyes crinkle up at the corners. If Tara were conscious, I know she'd be getting all wet about that.

"Maybe I will have that beer," says Chris.

I nod, grab one out of the mini fridge, and hand it over, watch as she opens it and takes a long swig.

"Hey," Chris says, "did you ever find out what the deal was with your boss?"

"Oh yeah," I answer. I am propped up on one elbow now, again tracing the curve of Tara's thigh with my hand. "She was just having a bad day. Nothing to do with me."

"You were so worried."

"I know."

I move my hand higher, up under Tara's skirt, watching Chris's face as I do it. Her eyes widen. I smile.

"You think her skin is soft, you should feel her lips."

Chris raises her eyebrows and smirks at my hand all up under Tara's skirt.

"No," I say, taking Chris's fingers and touching them gently to Tara's mouth. "These lips."

Tara, feeling the pressure of Chris's fingers, frowns and turns her face to the side. My eyes never leave Chris's as I lean over and press my mouth to Tara's, forcing her lips apart with my tongue. I probe the warm depths of her mouth, working my fat tongue like a cock. When I finally pull away, my eyes still locked with

Chris's, Tara's soft lips make a wet smacking sound. Chris stares at me in silence, wondering what will happen next. "Your turn," I say, at last. "Kiss her."

As if hypnotized, Chris leans over and carefully places her lips over Tara's. She doesn't open her mouth.

"Come on." I try not to sound impatient. "Really kiss her. You know how I mean."

I see Chris's tongue slide between Tara's lips. After a moment, Chris pulls away, breathing fast and hard. No way she's not turned on as all hell. I feel like some kind of fucking philanthropist, dispensing to the needy.

"You want more than that, don't you?" Chris hesitates, then nods. "Go on," I say like it's nothing, "Touch her breasts."

"But she's out cold."

"Not like she's dead."

"No, I mean, what if she doesn't want me to?"

"She told me she did."

"Still, I can't—"

"Why not?" I deadpan. "Don't you know how?"

"Oh, I know how."

Still Chris hesitates, a tense sweat prickling its way across her upper lip. I start to unbutton Tara's shirt.

"There. Aren't they fucking beautiful?" I reach over and undo the front clasp of Tara's bra. Her perfect breasts are luminous in the soft bedside light. Chris's intake of breath is audible. "Go on," I say, cranked up on the orders I'm giving. "Use your mouth."

And Chris does. Sure she pauses first, uncertain, but then some instinct overtakes her. Her lips tug one of Tara's pink nipples into her mouth, her hand reaches up automatically to pinch Tara's other nipple. Tara shifts a little, and a sigh escapes her lips. Now Chris cups

Tara's breasts with both hands, squeezing them together, running her tongue back and forth between the two erect nipples.

"Yo, easy there, Buddy. You'd think you hadn't seen a nice pair of tits in months. You'd think you hadn't fucked in years. Wait, you and Cathy do fuck, don't you? Never mind, don't tell me, I don't want to picture it."

Chris turns away from Tara and looks warily at me. She takes another pull of her beer. I can tell she's wondering if she should be insulted, but she's too curious about what will happen next.

"I'm just playing." I reach over to twist Tara's wet nipple between my fingers. "I know you know how to fuck. I'm sure you give it to sweet Cathy good. Right?"

Chris doesn't respond.

"Or isn't she enough for you?" My voice is low, coaxing. "Chris, do you want to fuck Tara?"

Chris doesn't answer; she's studying the rim of her beer bottle.

"What about it? Want a crack at her?'

Chris stares at me. "What are you saying?" Her voice is hoarse.

"What do you think I'm saying?" I lean forward and cover one of Tara's nipples with my mouth. After a half a second, Chris does the same. When I finally pull away, Chris is still sucking on Tara's hard nipple, desperate, like a hungry baby. She doesn't look up until she hears the snaps of Tara's jean skirt opening. I leave the skirt beneath Tara like the towel I put under her when she has her period and I want to see my dick sliding in and out of her blood-slicked hole.

"I think you're saying you want to pimp out your girlfriend." Chris watches my face.

"Nah," I say, like the cocky asshole I am. "You don't have to pay me anything this time."

I tug the crotch of Tara's black lace panties away from her pussy so Chris can get a good look at Tara's dark hair.

"Touch her."

"No. I mean, isn't that like rape or something?" Chris looks uncomfortable. She's sweating even more now. She smells greasy like the burgers we had for dinner and her face is red.

"It's not rape," I scoff. "She told me she wants it. Hell, she even told you."

Tara was drunk when she said it, but Chris remembers it, too.

"Look, I own her and I say you can touch her." I sit up, lean towards Chris. "I say you can fuck her."

I jerk Tara's panties all the way to the side and jam two of my fingers up inside of her. To my surprise she's wet. Maybe she's not out cold after all. Either that or, even unconscious she wants it, hot bitch.

"Come on," I say to Chris, moving my fingers in and out. "She feels so good inside."

Chris doesn't move.

"Think you're too out of practice to give it to her, right?"

"No." Chris finally meets my challenge. "I'm not."

She gets up and moves to the end of the bed. The next thing I know she has Tara's underwear down around her ankles and her face is buried in Tara's hot pussy.

I stand back and watch my friend eating my girlfriend. It's making me hot, but it's also making me mad. Although still asleep, Tara begins to wriggle underneath Chris's tongue. She moans softly and I see her hands grip at the sheets beneath her. Meanwhile, Chris laps Tara like some kind of crazed bulldog. She can't get enough of Tara's snatch. Not that I blame her.

"Yeah . . ." I say softly, "That's right Chris, eat her. Get your tongue in that hot hole. Eat her, man."

Chris moans and mashes her face harder into Tara's wet pussy. She looks like she's gonna swallow Tara whole. She looks like she's eating the best-tasting pussy ever, which, of course, she is. Now Tara is thrusting her hips a little, rubbing her sopping cunt against Chris's feverish face. Suddenly I'm hot as hell. I pull my sweatshirt over my head and use the bottom of my wife-beater to wipe the sweat from my neck. I'm getting so turned on and pissed off I don't know whether to smack Chris in the jaw and haul her the hell off of my girlfriend, or push her face deeper into Tara's pussy.

"All right," I say, when I just can't take it anymore. "Get the fuck off."

Chris looks up, dazed, a wolf poised over his kill. Her face is gleaming with Tara's juices.

"Enough," I say. "Let's fuck her."

It's no secret that I like to sport a hard-on every now and then, and tonight I've come prepared. I unbutton my jeans and release my harness-secured dick. Slowly I roll on a lube-slicked condom. Nudging Chris out of the way, I kneel on the bed between Tara's spread legs. I position the head of my cock at her opening, all sloppy wet from Chris's mouth. Hoisting Tara's legs over my shoulders, I plunge my cock into her hot hole. Tara's body jolts, and she lets out a squeak.

"That's right, baby," I say, working it in, "take it. I don't care if you're awake or asleep, conscious or unconscious, dead or alive, you're gonna take this big cock."

I keep pumping her, hard. I know Chris is there, I know she's watching, but all I can think is how much I need to fuck Tara. Finally I pull out, peel off the condom, and turn to face Chris. She's breathing heavily, her hand groping unthinkingly at the crotch of her pants. She wants a dick of her own. She's in luck.

I toss her one. It's a little bit smaller than mine, but come on—we all know no one's gonna be bigger than me.

"Here," I say. "I don't have another harness, but just—"

Before I can finish instructing her, she's already tucked the cock into her fly, and is fastening the buttons around the base to hold it in place.

"You take her pussy," I say generously. "I'll take her mouth."

Immediately Chris pulls Tara to the edge of the bed. Standing over her, she rubs her dick over Tara's slit before stuffing it in her hole. I straddle Tara's face and force her mouth open with my cock. Tara murmurs and tries to turn her head away.

"Uh-uh." I say, "No fucking way. You're going to take this big dick all the way down your pretty little throat." I begin to thrust in and out of Tara's mouth. She's coughing a bit now, and tears are oozing out of her closed eyes. At the other end of the bed, Chris is fucking the shit out of my girlfriend's tight pussy. Chris's making all sorts of guttural groaning noises, really getting into it.

"Yeah," Chris says. "Yeah, you know you want it. Come on, slut."

I can't believe my ears, but somehow I always knew Chris had it in her. My dick is hitting the back of Tara's throat, and the base is bumping against my clit. Any minute, I'm gonna blow. Chris looks like she's on the edge herself. I'm not ready for this to end though. Not by a long shot.

"Chris," I command, "stop."

"Wha—?" Chris looks confused, worried I've had a change of heart.

I lie down next to Tara and gesture for Chris to lie down, too. I shift Tara's used body toward me and position myself again between her legs. It's hard work this time; she's wide open, but dry inside. I have to force it. Finally my dick is in up to the hilt, and I'm grinding my pelvis against Tara's. I'm just letting the buzzing feeling in my clit grow to a crescendo when Tara's body is jerked away from me.

"Dude," says Chris, "give someone else a chance."

She turns Tara to face her and begins to piston her rod in and out of Tara's helpless body. I give Chris a couple of minutes and then pull Tara back to me. Tara's eyes are still closed but she is beginning to make small, peeping objections.

"No," she says softly, "no, please!"

"I don't hear any damn safe word," I murmur, clapping a hand over Tara's mouth, continuing to pound her. I notice that Chris has one hand on Tara's waist and the other . . . I slow my rhythm for a moment and peer over Tara's shoulder. Chris's other hand is parting Tara's smooth, round ass cheeks.

Did I say I was feeling generous? Not when it comes to Tara's ass. I'm the first person to fuck that virgin opening. Before me Tara couldn't take a pinky finger up in there, but I trained her. I've got her taking three fingers in that hole and begging for more. I've never fucked her with a cock as big as the one I'm wearing, though. Never even fucked her with one the size that Chris has on. I'm as generous as the next guy, but if you think I'm going to let someone else be the first to ream my girlfriend's ass, you're smoking some deadly weed.

"No fucking way, Chris," I say, rolling Tara over again.

"I can't wait," Chris groans. "I just need to fuck her."

"You take her cunt, then. Leave her ass to me."

"Whatever." Chris barely gets the word out before she's inside Tara's swollen pussy. I pull Tara's ass cheeks apart and run my finger up and down her crack. She's slightly moist back there, but there's no way she can take a dick like mine without a few squirts of lube. But the lube is all the way at the other end of the bed inside my backpack. Fuck it, I can't wait that long. Holding her ass open with one hand, I use the other to position my dick. Tara grunts as I force the head inside of her. I swear I can feel Tara's asshole tear, as the head of my rod rams through her tight sphincter. Yes. I'm in. Tara's moans have become screams now, and all I want is to shoot my fucking wad. I move in and out of Tara's ass. I can feel Chris's tool through the thin membrane that separates us. Tara's wordless screaming is really getting to me. I'm going to come any second. I slap her ass.

"Shut the fuck up," I say through clenched teeth. "That's right, slut, just let us fucking use you, little fuck doll."

At that moment, Chris groans and starts to shake. "Yeah," she says, "Yeah, Tara, milk it." Suddenly I'm over the edge. I come like a fucking madman, shaking and thrusting all over the place. When I'm done, I see that somehow, just like in Hollywood, Chris has finished at the same time. We withdraw from Tara's trembling body. Tara curls her legs to her chest and moans. Chris looks dazed.

"Hey," I say quietly, "why don't you hit the shower, give the happy couple a few minutes alone?"

"All right." Chris wanders off toward the bathroom. I zip up, take a look at Tara. She has bite marks all over her neck. The pale, clear skin on her back and thighs is already purpling with bruises.

"You awake, baby?"

No response. I tug the nubby, tan blanket over her, and curl my body around hers. Next thing I know my head is being split nearly open by a shaft of light through the curtains.

"You were sleeping like the dead." Tara stands in front of me, hair still wet from the shower. "You're not going to believe this," she says, sitting gingerly on the edge of the mattress, "and please don't be mad. It's not like you aren't amazing in bed, and normally I would totally remember every moment, but I think I had too much to drink last night and . . ." She pauses. "Well, I have no idea what happened. We did have sex, right? We must have because I'm really sore, but I just don't remember. You're not mad, are you?'

I laugh. "Of course I'm not mad."

"Oh, good." Tara smiles and reaches for her hairbrush. "Hmm," she says. "What's this, a note?"

I hold my hand out for the folded up piece of paper she's found on the nightstand. "*Thanks.—Chris.*"

"Did Chris come up after the bar?" Tara asks.

"Yeah, she hung out for a while."

"Shit! I can't believe I missed that."

"Don't worry," I say, "you'll get to see your boyfriend again soon."

"She's not my boyfriend. She's Cathy's." Tara makes a face. "Although what Chris sees in that sexless little decoupage-er, I will never know."

"Chris says she's sweet."

"What's Chris thanking you for, anyway?" Tara asks, maybe a touch too innocently.

I can't help it. I smirk and stroke Tara's cheek with the back of my hand.

"Something I gave her."

THE DAY THE SUN GODDESS GOT LAID

DONNA GEORGE STOREY

HER AUGUSTNESS HEAVENLY-ALARMING FEMALE lay a sounding board before the door of the rock dwelling (where Amaterasu Omikami, She Who Is Heaven Shining, was in retreat). She stamped on it until she made a sound in a wild and frenzied manner as if possessed, and she pulled the nipples of her breasts out and pushed down her skirt string and exposed her private parts. Then the Plain of High Heaven shook and the eight hundred Deities laughed together.

—*Records of Ancient Matters,* Japan, AD 680

WHY DID THEY *laugh?*

Amaterasu, Supreme Goddess of the Plain of High Heaven, closed her eyes and lay back on the bed she'd fashioned from her thousand-layer kimono. She would discover the answer. She would not leave the sanctuary of this cave until she did.

Outside, the pounding grew louder, more desperate. The High Council of Japanese Deities had called upon the God of Strength to beat his great fists against the boulder she had rolled across the opening of the cave. No one was laughing now.

"Come out, Great Shining One, we entreat you! We've been too long without your light. The mortals on the Reed Plain below are wailing with fear. We will do anything to appease your wrath."

If only they would go away and leave me alone.

Not all the eight hundred myriad Deities could move her with their pleas. It was indeed rage—and confusion—that had brought her to shut herself away in this place, but those feelings had already melted into the sultry air of the cave. She found that she was beginning to enjoy solitude.

The world beyond might be plunged into darkness, but Amaterasu's retreat glowed like an oven. The walls of the cave sweated a pearly dew, fragrant as new bread.

The Shining One herself felt beads of moisture rise on her skin. Seeking relief, she stripped off her thousand robes one by one, the rosy hues of dawn tangled together with the deep ochres and indigos of sunset, until all that remained was bare golden flesh.

Amaterasu blushed at first to behold her unclothed form, but then her lips curved into a smile. She had never done such a thing before. Baths in the Tranquil River of Heaven were hurried affairs, her handmaidens shielding her from any untoward gaze with screens of silver clouds. Until now, the goddess, too, had turned her eyes away from her own nakedness. Partly from modesty, yes, but there were so many other things to observe in her realm below as she journeyed across the sky each day.

In this place, however, there was nothing to gaze upon but the terrain of her own flesh, rising up over her breasts, then sloping down into a shimmering meadow of grasses that narrowed between her gilded thighs like a dancing girl's fan.

The vision made her lightheaded, as if she had drunk deep from a vat of sacred rice wine. She brought her hands to her chest—to calm herself at first. But then her fingers began to wander over her breasts, circling, stroking, and pinching the pointed tips, which blushed deep rose like the mountain peaks at dawn.

Her hands traveled down over her belly. She felt a throbbing there, as if a smaller, hotter cave was hidden away within her.

Outside the knocking and pleading started up once more. "Great Shining One, we beseech you! The High Council has exiled your brother. He will trouble you no more."

Her brother's unruly acts were indeed one reason she had locked herself away, but Amaterasu only sniffed at the news. Her hands continued their journey, ever lower through the meadow of silken thread to the cleft between her legs. Her fingertip ventured into the dewy vale. Why did her face feel so hot now? Why did her thighs fall open of their own accord?

Amaterasu caught her breath when she found *it*, a small jewel swathed in the silky softness of the crevice. The Heavens must hold magic even she did not know. How else could it be that one touch sent hot, jagged lightning bolts all through her body?

She touched the jewel again. And again. Her nimble master

weaver's fingers began to dance over it, as they did at her sacred loom, conjuring a tapestry of sensation that rippled through her. Her flesh was white-hot now, the radiance swelling to fill the cave.

"Her beams shine through the stone in a golden crown of light," the voices cried. "She is coming. Heaven and Earth will be saved."

Lost as she was in her pleasure, Amaterasu had to smile at their foolish words. Her fingers slowed. The corona of light around her faded from the blinding yellow of high summer to winter's pale fire.

No, she was not coming yet. Not until she had her answer. She knew now it was within her grasp.

◆

HOW LONG HAD IT BEEN since she began her ascent of the vault of Heaven without a troubled heart? Each day her golden eyes roamed the land below, warming the backs of the sinewy laborers scything grain and fishermen hauling in nets swollen with thrashing fish. But it was the women, her subjects fashioned in her own lovely image, who made her pause in her journey. She watched mothers carrying babies on their hips, pressing their noses to their tiny heads to breathe in the clean scent of grain and milk. She gazed upon maidens washing clothes in the streams, their robes hiked over their opalescent thighs. And, now and then —although her twin brother, the moon, was said to enjoy this sight far more often—she spied a woman giving herself to a man's embrace.

Amaterasu stared, the blush of evening settling on her cheeks, as the man kissed the woman's lips and neck, then pulled her robe from her shoulders to uncover her breasts. Some men would only gaze for a while, making a sound of pleasure as if sitting down to a fine supper. Some would caress the creamy demi-globes, or toy with the nipples like a child, then, childlike still, bend to suckle.

After a time—sometimes brief, sometimes long—the man would pull away his loincloth to reveal his own secret, a ruddy rod of flesh rearing up from between his thighs. He would push this rod between the woman's bared legs where, by some trick, it disappeared. The two bodies moved together as if in some strange dance. *Did it hurt to have that thing inside you*? Amaterasu wondered. She had many children, but they'd been born from her broken sword, and her sacred jewels, and the mist of her breath.

She studied the faces of the women as they lay beneath the men, or bent over them from above, or crouched on all fours to be entered from behind. Some did indeed seem pained, their mouths set in a grim line, but others set to wailing and moaning in way that did not sound at all sad. A few, and this was the strangest of all, would laugh out loud.

Why?

Each morning Amaterasu rose, determined to unravel this mystery. Yet, day after day, no answer came. The other gods kept their distance from the Great Shining One, and no mortal would dare presume to court her. After midnight, when she'd finished weaving stars of silver thread onto the night sky, she would retire alone to her private pavilion while the other gods gathered to drink saké and dance. Some were so heedless in their lust, they took their pleasure outside her very door, grunting together like beasts. But Amaterasu could no more be one with them than with the tiny mortals on the Reed Plain far below.

She was the goddess of all that was light, but inside she was only darkness.

Then came the day her spirited brother, Susano-o the Storm God, ascended to Heaven to pay his respects. For the next few days, Amaterasu almost forgot her loneliness. Laughing and reeking of saké, Susano-o would pull his sister from her loom to join in the celestial revelry. He kept her wine cup full and told her ribald jokes that, the other gods were astounded to observe, made her grave eyes gleam and her stately mouth curve ever-so-slightly upward in amusement.

But her brother gave Amaterasu another gift that she spoke of to no one. She'd been on her way back from the bath, when she saw him—them—running through the forest. A minor deity, the guardian of spring flowers, raced into the sacred grove with Susano-o in thundering pursuit. One gust from his mighty lungs sent her pastel robes flying up around her waist to expose her rosy buttocks and stemlike legs. The goddess cried out and stopped to cover herself, an unfortunate gesture, as it allowed the Storm God to catch her and pull her to the ground. He pawed at the young deity's body, all the while feasting on her soft neck and small breasts with greedy, lapping sounds.

Frozen to the spot, Amaterasu could only watch as Susano-o wedged his knees between his captive's legs and wrenched them open. Impetuous as he was, he immediately drew his maleness from his robes: a purple truncheon that made Amaterasu wince. It was then she resolved to help the maiden, but just as she stepped forward, the flower guardian sat up, beheld her brother's weapon, and began to giggle. Still laughing, she extended a dainty hand to touch it. Amaterasu withdrew to the shadows of an ancient tree and stared as the small hand grasped the ruddy stalk and rubbed it up and down from the root to its domed, bulging head. Susano-o, who had never been quiet or still since his birth from his father's sneeze, simply knelt there under her caresses, still as stone. Tears of rain seeped down his cheeks—and, as if in sympathy, a few more wept from the smaller eye at the tip of his lordly member.

As the Shining One gazed, transfixed, the flower goddess grew bolder. She pushed the Storm God back on the ground and lowered herself onto that fearsome cylinder of flesh. A soft howl rose from Susano-o's lips as the goddess arched and shook in the mating dance. A nameless sound came forth from her throat, too, not a song, not a sigh. If pressed, Amaterasu would have to say the flower goddess was laughing.

Why?

That night Amaterasu refused to join in the party. She sat in her pavilion, questions whirling through her head until the stars winked out one by one in preparation for her ascent. She was not like her brother; that much she knew. Yet the vision of his coupling with the flower guardian still throbbed inside her. Like hunger. Like pain.

Feeling bored and slighted by his melancholy sister, it was then Susano-o began his mischief. He blustered through the Heavens, breaking down the rice canals and vomiting in the Sacred Shrine. Amaterasu excused him by saying he'd drunk too much saké, though she knew the other gods disapproved of her indulgence.

Her kindness seemed to enrage him all the more. "Maybe this will get a rise out of you," he bellowed as he hurled a flayed colt right through the roof of the hall where Amaterasu and her handmaidens wove the night sky.

The weaver maids screamed and scattered, but one of her favorites, a fragile goddess as white as porcelain, was caught beneath a fallen loom, sending her to the underworld for eternity. Shaking with sorrow, the Shining One could not confront her brother with his terrible deeds even now. For in truth, the skinless corpse of the colt reminded her all too keenly of the moist red cleft of the flower guardian, so rudely exposed as she lay with Susano-o on a bed of leaves in the forest.

Her face blazing orange with rage and shame, Amaterasu rushed to the cave on the banks of the Tranquil River of Heaven and rolled the boulder door across the opening.

Now all of Heaven and Earth dwelled in the same darkness that troubled her heart.

◆

AMATERASU SAT UP and tilted an ear toward the door of the cave. Voices rose up again, louder than before, but this time there was no pleading or lamentation. The myriad deities were cheering and calling out a name.

"Uzumé, the Whirling One, Heaven's Forthright Female, give us a show!"

The Shining One frowned. Had her subjects forgotten her so soon? She had made wondrous discoveries in her solitude, but part of her longed to join in the merrymaking once more.

The pounding started slowly, echoing throughout the Heavens.

"Faster, Whirling One! Faster!"

Amaterasu understood then it was no drum. Uzumé was dancing, playing the floor of the wooden stage with her feet. She had seen this Forthright Female, Goddess of Mirth and Playfulness, dance to the music of her brother's sighs a few brief nights ago. She saw her now, her figure flickering against the cave wall, almost too bright to be mere memory. Uzumé's wild black hair falling to her knees. Her generous crimson mouth. Her skirt riding scandalously low on her broad hips. Amaterasu could even smell her: musk, seawater, and a smoky, honeyed scent, like broiled sweetish.

"Show us your tits, Uzumé!"

The Shining One recognized the nasal voice of Sarutahiko, the Phallic God. His very long, red nose had a bulbous tip that made Amaterasu think of a misshapen mushroom. She always averted her gaze when their paths met.

"Holy Heaven, she's actually doing it," came the voice of a goddess, hoarse with excitement. "How can she shake them round and round like that? There's a trick I'd like to learn."

A chorus of deeper voices joined in. "That's it, play with your own nipples. Are they big enough you can suck 'em yourself? What else have you got for us, Uzumé? Look at what I have for you—you're making me hard as a rock!"

Amaterasu moved closer to the cave door. Impulsively, she gathered her robes around her body and tied the sash in a makeshift knot.

"She's not taking off her skirt, is she? Even that hussy wouldn't go so far!"

Amaterasu rested her hand on the boulder. She wanted to see Uzumé's lewd show so badly she was trembling.

"There goes the skirt. I can't believe it—now she's spreading her legs. She's touching herself, holding her nether lips open so all can see . . ."

Suddenly the Heavens erupted, a torrent of sound crashing against the boulder at the door of the cave. Shrill female cries rose in waves above the rolling thunder of male jollity. It took the sun goddess a few moments to understand what it was: all eight hundred myriad deities were laughing.

What was so goddamn funny?

Amaterasu nudged the rock aside and peeked out.

A vision shimmered before her, suspended in midair amidst the thick branches of the Heavenly Sakaki Tree. It was the image of a woman, lips parted in surprise. Her oval face gleamed a dark, burnished gold, her glossy hair tumbled around her shoulders in voluptuous disarray. Amaterasu pushed the boulder aside a few inches more. Now she glimpsed the woman's resplendent body, draped in a kimono of a thousand hues, which fell suggestively over one smooth shoulder.

The Shining One brought her hand to her cheek. The woman did the same.

Amaterasu let her fingertips slide down to touch her chest, where the breasts began to swell. The woman floating in the tree did the same. Her eyes, gazing steadily back, glimmered with secret pleasure. The smaller, hotter cave deep in Amaterasu's belly began to glow once more.

She was ready to come out.

Japanese legend tells that the Shining One was indeed tricked into coming out of seclusion when she saw her reflection in a mirror hung in the sacred tree. But Amaterasu was never really fooled. She knew she was gazing at her own face. Yet how different that visage was from the timid, wavering reflection she had seen during her ablutions in the Tranquil River of Heaven. This woman in the mirror knew dark, hidden secrets. She was beautiful.

"Why?" the Shining One murmured. "Why are you all making such an ungodly noise?"

Naked but for a gossamer shift of sweat glittering like jewels, Uzumé jumped from the stage and hurried to her mistress. She gestured to the image of the woman floating in the tree. "We are celebrating, Shining One, because we have seen a new goddess who is more illustrious than you."

Amaterasu stepped out of the cave, only dimly aware that the God of Strength rolled the boulder back into place behind her and bolted it fast with iron braces. She fixed her gaze on Uzumé —*if only that impudent dancer knew how right she was*—a frown clouding her features.

"You have disturbed me in my rest." Her voice resounded through the Heavens, and all of the eight hundred myriad deities sputtered apologies and fell prostrate to the ground. All but one. Uzumé remained standing, biting her lip to hold back a smile.

Amaterasu drew herself to her full height. "And you, Forthright Female, the most brazen of all my subjects." She paused, as if she were deciding which punishment would be most terrible and fitting. "I will speak with you alone."

Uzumé hung her head—in fear or to hide a smile?—and followed her mistress into the sacred grove not far from the river's edge.

Once they were alone, Amaterasu whirled around to face the dancer. "Uzumé! I want you to show me exactly what you did on stage."

"Shining One," the Forthright Female protested, "if that is what you desire, I must return and put on my robe and skirt for that is how I began the dance."

"I don't care about that part of it." Amaterasu faltered. "The voices, back there, they said . . . you touched your own breasts . . . and you bared yourself below . . ." She found she could not continue.

"I did do these things as I danced, Shining One." Uzumé raised her head and looked straight into Amaterasu's eyes. "But now I would much rather show you another dance. It requires two."

Amaterasu let out a whimper of surprise as the dancer grasped her hands and pressed them to her naked, sweat-slick bosom. Uzumé's breasts were larger than her own, the flesh spilling over her hands. The dark nipples were as round as the saucers upon which the celestial handmaidens served dainties. So different from her own and yet, when Amaterasu rolled the tips between her fingers, the tips stood up like little knobs, just as hers did now beneath her kimono.

"Ah, I see I have no need to show you anything, Shining One. What secrets did you discover when you were in that cave?" Uzumé gave her a sly look, but soon enough she seemed to forget her question, as her head lolled back and her breath quickened.

Amaterasu grew bolder, exploring the dancer's body at her will. Uzumé's lower meadow was thicker, the coarse grasses tickling her fingers in an oddly pleasant fashion. But as the Shining One's fingers parted the lips and sought the silk-swathed jewel, the vision was suddenly familiar, as if she were looking in a dusky mirror, the reflection darker, though nonetheless true.

She stroked the hard little nugget, which seemed to swell against the tireless attentions of her finger. Soon Uzumé's legs began to tremble. With a cry, the dancer fell to her knees, panting. "It is too soon for the dance to end, Shining One. First there's another step I must show you. May I part your August robes?"

Amaterasu gazed at Uzumé's upturned face, the playful grin, the sparkling eyes. The Forthright Female knew the secret. Uzumé knew exactly why they laughed.

And so Amaterasu pulled aside her thousand robes of every hue and tilted her hips forward to accept the homage of the dancer's satin tongue.

Now she did know for certain that the Plain of High Heaven held more magic than she had ever fathomed. How else could the dance of Uzumé's tongue send answering tongues of flame licking up through her belly, the heat turning to a steady drumbeat of desire? The pounding inside her grew faster and louder. Amaterasu's knees gave way and she sank to the ground.

Uzumé knelt above her now, her lips and chin glistening. "You are so beautiful down there, Shining One," she whispered, "like folds of shimmering golden cloth. And you taste like a ripe peach from the Garden of Eternal Summer."

So, this is what it means to be seen, to be loved.

Amaterasu reached up and touched Uzumé's cheek. "Let me see you. Let me taste you."

Uzumé turned and straddled the sun goddess' glowing face.

Amaterasu's lungs ached with Uzumé's smoky-sweet perfume; her lips sucked in her wetness. Timidly she sought out the secret jewel with the tip of her tongue. The way Uzumé began to jerk her hips and moan in a most forthright manner told her she had found it.

This is what it means to dance.

Uzumé bent forward, nestling her face between Amaterasu's thighs. It was then the duet began in earnest: Uzumé's tongue twirling, whirling, tapping. Amaterasu tried her best to mimic her teacher, but soon her body seemed to move of its own accord.

Her belly ignited with a column of fire that filled her torso and poured through her mouth into Uzumé's body, only to be fed back again by the dancer's skillful moves. One above and one below, mirroring each other in a pulsing circle of gold.

This is what I want inside me. This is what I wanted all along.

Uzumé's tongue grew more frenzied. Her hips swayed and shook. Urgent and hungry, Amaterasu spread her own legs wider and pushed up against the dancer's mouth.

That's when it happened.

The feeling came in waves, a huge, hot fist squeezing her insides over and over again. She knew, with all her being, that this explosion of light inside her was Heaven's greatest bounty. And the sound she made then was not dainty, neither song nor sigh.

For the first time, though it would not be the last, Amaterasu, Supreme Goddess of the Plain of High Heaven, laughed.

THE PERFECT FIT

STEPHANIE ROSE

LORREN DROVE UP to the nondescript two-story building and parked right out front. Plain gray stone with plain white trim made the understated building blend in with the others on the block.

She checked the piece of paper resting on the passenger's seat. Yeah, this was the right address, she thought. Her friend Anita had recommended this place over a month ago, but Lorren wasn't the least bit interested. Now she was at least ready to try.

She checked her reflection in her rear-view mirror. She shook out her thick auburn hair, styled in an easy, swinging bob. She stroked her cinnamon-colored skin. Not bad, she sighed as she admired herself from different angles. At least it's much better than before. At least I'm no longer hideous, she thought.

Hands shaking, she got out of the car and pressed the button for the intercom. Waiting, she frowned as she looked at her reflection in the glass door. Her loose gray sweater and simple white denim skirt had once been one of her favorite outfits, but not anymore. Today, all she could see was the dated look of the plain garments.

Lorren's figure was lean, but she pinched her waist anyway and snorted in disgust at the extra bit of flesh she felt there. The usual butterflies in her stomach fluttered as what seemed like an eternity passed. Finally, a deep, yet sensual feminine voice boomed over the intercom.

"Yes?"

Lorren's voice shook. "Hi. I'm Lorren Tate. I have an appointment?"

"Hi, Lorren. Come on up to the second floor."

A buzzer went off and the door unlocked. As Lorren walked in, she was immediately greeted with the sight and scent of an assortment of vanilla candles. In addition, tiny tea lights placed around the room also gave the area a soft, warm glow.

The lower level of the building reminded Lorren of an upscale lounge; it was furnished with a soft black leather sofa and loveseat in the center and had small tables and plush chairs around the perimeter. An expensive Oriental rug lay over beautifully finished hardwood floors. This would be a great place to entertain, Lorren thought. At one point, she loved to throw parties and have friends over, but recent events in her life made that impossible. She sighed heavily, a wave of sadness suddenly rushing over her.

Lorren spotted the staircase in the corner of the room. As she climbed up, her palms began to sweat. Nervous, she unconsciously wiped them on her skirt. "Oh, shit," she said as she instantly realized her mistake. Her handprints left marks on the white fabric. "Damn it," she grumbled. "I can be so careless sometimes."

She sighed as she continued up the stairs, but when she reached the landing, she was surprised to see strands of scarlet beads hanging from the upstairs doorway. As she parted them and stepped in, she gasped, awestruck at what she saw.

In and around the room were racks and racks of the silkiest and sexiest lingerie Lorren had ever seen.

Corsets were positioned across from bra-and-panty sets. Silk robes and sheer nighties were located right next to silk teddies. Scores of sexy stockings and garter belts were displayed in glass cases throughout the shop. Several colorful feather boas were also draped around the room.

Lorren also noticed that the mannequins in this store had various sizes and shapes—very different from the usual mannequins she saw. That put her a bit at ease.

"Welcome, my dear," Lorren heard the sensual voice say. She turned to see a tall, slender woman stride gracefully from the back of the shop.

The exotic woman had soft, smooth, kissable skin the color of rich, dark espresso. Her stunning almond-shaped eyes were highlighted with smoky black and brown shades. Her bright and pretty smile was decorated with a vibrant berry lipcolor. Her jet-black hair hung in loose waves well down her back. Her nails were artfully manicured and her neck, wrists, and fingers were adorned with delicate gold jewelry. She wore a black lace wrap dress that hit above her knee, showing off her toned calves. Four-inch, jet-black heels gave her legs the ultimate sleek and sexy look.

"Hi, Lorren. I'm Miss Lila. Welcome to Summer Rose Lingerie."

By this time, Lorren's face was beet red. She couldn't believe that she'd stared at the woman that long. She quickly composed herself. "Hi, Miss Lila." She looked around. "You have a very nice place here. But I have to admit: I'm not too sure about this . . ."

Miss Lila held out her hand. "Come. Sit." She gently led Lorren to a set of leather chairs in the center of the room.

"Is anyone else here?" Lorren asked.

"No. This is a private appointment. We're the only ones here." Miss Lila took a seat directly across from Lorren and looked into her timid brown eyes. She quickly read Lorren's apprehension and decided to be upfront about it. "Now, why are you so nervous? Are you uncomfortable here?" Miss Lila asked.

"No, I'm not nervous," Lorren said abruptly. "I'm just not sure if this is for me." Lorren looked over and spotted a gold string bikini hanging on one of the display racks. A vision of herself in the bikini flashed in her mind. Ugh, she thought. "No. This place isn't for me."

"Why not?"

"This stuff—" Lorren waved her hand around. "—this stuff is for . . . other women. Not me." She suddenly grabbed her purse. "I have to go. I'm sorry if I've wasted your time."

"Lorren, why are you so tense? You're gorgeous. And you deserve beautiful, luxurious things just like anyone else."

"No," Lorren protested. "Don't say that."

"It's true." Miss Lila reached out to gently stroke Lorren's cheek. "You're a beautiful woman, Lorren."

"You say that now," Lorren said. "But you wouldn't have said that a year ago . . ."

"Why not?" Miss Lila asked.

Lorren fell silent, but she balled her fists tightly.

"Lorren? Why not?"

"It's because I was . . . heavier back then," Lorren whispered.

"Heavier?"

Lorren sighed. "Not too long ago, I was over a hundred pounds overweight."

"Tell me about it, Lorren," Miss Lila pressed.

Lorren hesitated, but Miss Lila's expression was filled with such caring and such concern that she decided to risk it.

"Well, here's the short version: My dad died a few years ago and I think I just ate myself into oblivion. I was so sad that I really didn't care about myself anymore. I didn't watch my diet and I rarely exercised. But eventually I just got sick of it. I felt horrible because I was always sluggish. And nothing fit me anymore. And I was so unhappy."

Miss Lila gently stroked Lorren's hand. She then reached out and tenderly tucked a loose strand of Lorren's hair back behind her ear.

Loving Miss Lila's gentle touch, Lorren's voice grew stronger. "So I decided that I had to change. I had to free myself. Not just free myself from the weight, but free myself from treating myself so carelessly. So I decided that even if I never lost a pound, I would at least watch what I ate and work out on a regular basis. And as I felt better, I kept going. And it eventually worked out."

"How long did it take?"

"Just over a year."

"Well, congratulations on your effort," Miss Lila said. "You look beautiful now. But I have to be honest: I personally believe that every woman is gorgeous, no matter what her size. And I believe it's my job to make every woman see that she has the right to be glamorous and sexy and confident. So even though you didn't think so, I'm sure that you looked gorgeous back then as well."

"No, I didn't," Lorren admitted.

"I find that hard to believe," Miss Lila answered. "For example, don't you know that you have an amazing bone structure? And a drop-dead gorgeous smile? And stunning legs?"

Lorren's shoulders relaxed and she chuckled. "Now you're just trying to sell me lingerie."

"Yes," Miss Lila laughed. "That may be true. But I'm more interested in selling you some self-esteem."

Lorren's head snapped. "Excuse me? What did you say?"

"Easy, hon," Miss Lila said smoothly. "I didn't mean to rattle you. But I do believe in being blunt. And, to put it bluntly, you need to feel better about yourself."

Miss Lila held out her hand. "Will you let me help you?"

Lorren paused. This woman was seductive as hell but borderline rude. Lorren looked down at her loose, baggy sweater. She even noticed the fraying around the sleeves. Who was she kidding? Her wardrobe was pitiful. Since her dramatic weight loss, most of her clothes didn't fit anymore, and the ones that did were seriously outdated. As her friend Anita suggested, having a professional lingerie fitting could be the perfect start to a whole new wardrobe. A whole new life, even.

"OK," Lorren whispered.

"Come with me."

Lorren followed Miss Lila to the rear of the shop. As they

reached the fitting area, Lorren noticed several carefully stacked boxes and neatly filed papers in the back workspace. She was immediately impressed at how tidy and orderly Miss Lila's shop was.

"Lorren, pick a fitting room, go inside, and take off your top."

"Excuse me?"

"I need to measure you, hon," Miss Lila assured. "So get comfy and I'll be back in a moment."

Lorren walked into one of the spacious fitting rooms. Reluctantly, she stripped off her sweater and faced the full-length mirrors. As she stood there, Miss Lila's words started to take effect. Lorren began to admire the sight of her slimmer arms and shoulders and realized that her arms looked great whether she was slim or not. However, the sight of her plain, white bra made her frown.

Suddenly, Lorren heard a soft knock.

"OK. I'm coming in," Miss Lila announced as she opened the door. She smiled as she admired Lorren's trim frame. "Very nice, Lorren. Now that you've told me that you're taking better care of yourself, I'd say that you've been working extremely hard. You should be proud."

Lorren blushed. "Thanks."

"OK. Lift up your arms, please," Miss Lila said. She wrapped a yellow measuring tape around Lorren's chest. "Hmmm . . ."

As she adjusted the tape, her hand accidentally brushed against Lorren's nipple. The flesh immediately hardened at Miss Lila's soft touch. Lorren turned scarlet red.

"Don't worry, hon," Miss Lila winked. "Happens all the time."

Lorren shook her head and lowered her eyes, mortified.

Wanting to spare the young woman further embarrassment, Miss Lila quickly took the last few measurements. "OK. All done." She wrapped up the measuring tape. "I'm going to grab something that I think is perfect for you and I'll be right back."

Lorren stood in front of the mirror looking at her shape. Well, it's not really bad, she thought. She turned to the side. I did work hard. And it's helped my overall life. Case in point: I have much more energy than before.

Miss Lila came back in, interrupting her thoughts. "OK, Lorren. Try this one first." She held up a scandalous leopard-print bra with dramatic black lace trim.

Lorren shook her head. "Oh, that's a bit much . . ."

"Don't be silly. It's perfect. It fits your new life. Risqué and wild." Miss Lila walked behind Lorren and quickly unclasped her bra. "Let me help you."

Before Lorren knew what was happening, Miss Lila whisked the fabric away and Lorren stood there nude from the waist up. Her firm breasts sagged just a bit, but the upper body exercises she'd done greatly improved how high they sat on her chest. Miss Lila's eyes were in the mirror, firmly locked on Lorren's cinnamon nipples.

Blushing, Lorren quickly slipped on the soft brassiere. Miss Lila reluctantly fastened the clasps.

Lorren looked at herself in the mirrors, stunned. "Wow." She was barely aware that the word slipped out of her mouth.

Lorren's soft brown skin was perfectly accented by the soft black-and-gold leopard-print fabric. The sturdy underwire cups of the bra gently lifted and separated Lorren's firm breasts, making them look luscious and inviting. The round, supple globes jiggled softly as Lorren turned in the mirror.

"See," Miss Lila said as they both admired Lorren's reflection. "You're a beautiful woman." Miss Lila gently placed her hand on

Lorren's shoulder. Lorren's breathing quickened as she felt Miss Lila's soft touch.

"OK. That one looks great. It fits you well," Miss Lila said. "Now try this one on next." She placed a jade green satin kimono on one of the hooks. "I'll be right back."

Lorren tilted her head as she looked at the satiny material. That isn't too bad, she thought. She unbuttoned her skirt and began to remove it. Then she glanced in the mirror and remembered the small pockets of flesh on the backs of her thighs. Suddenly bashful and forgetting her newly found confidence, she changed her mind and kept the skirt on as she wriggled into the satin kimono.

Lorren turned and scrutinized herself at every angle. Not able to find any obvious flaws, she finally relaxed and smiled at her reflection. Finally, she approved of her image in the mirror.

She playfully shook her hair and twirled around. "Rowr," Lorren growled, loving the feel of the cool, silky fabric. Giggling, she growled again, enjoying her animalistic impulses.

"Uh oh. Is there a wildcat in here?" Miss Lila teased as she came back into the fitting room.

Lorren giggled harder. "Meow," she purred.

"Ahhh. You like pussies," Miss Lila said.

All of a sudden, Lorren's face froze. She shook her head as she reached for her clothes. "I have to leave now. I'm not ready for this."

"Wait! I've offended you?" Miss Lila grasped Lorren's hand. "I'm sorry. Please don't be mad."

"No, no. Actually, it's OK," Lorren admitted. "I'm not offended. I'm not scared, either. I'm just a bit sensitive about that. See, it's just . . . it's just that I haven't had a girlfriend in quite a while."

"No?" Miss Lila perked up.

"No."

A moment passed and the twosome began to giggle. Lorren sighed and laid her head on Miss Lila's shoulder. The two ladies stood together, skin-to-skin, both silent and each drawing heat from the other.

Lorren finally spoke. "I've always loved girls. And I've dated a few. But after my dad died, I gained the weight so fast that I just stopped dating altogether." She frowned. "Girls stopped asking me out."

"Or maybe you started hiding?"

Lorren sighed. "Maybe . . ."

"Cheer up, hon. I have one more thing to show you. I'll be right back." Before she left, she pointed to the denim skirt that was still on Lorren's bottom half. "Oh, and would you take off your skirt, please? You have such beautiful legs." She winked as she shut the door.

Lorren's mouth dropped open. Oh, this was going way too far. *I should just put my clothes on and go.*

Suddenly, she realized that her present insecurities were giving her nothing but grief. A change had to be made or she'd never have true happiness again.

She carefully undressed, taking off the satin kimono, the leopard print bra, and her cotton panties. No longer bashful, she reveled in her nudity.

Her soft, round breasts jiggled as she moved. She studied her newly toned arms and legs and began to love and appreciate what she saw. She smiled at her dark, blazing eyes and smooth, silky brown skin. She even turned to appreciate her tight, firm ass. She silently gave thanks for her rich, African-American ancestry.

A knock at the door interrupted Lorren's thoughts.

"I have something extra special for you," Miss Lila announced.

She held up the final outfit, but once she caught sight of Lorren's nude body, she gasped. Miss Lila felt a raw need at the sight of Lorren's stunning physique. "You're beautiful, Lorren. I mean that." She regained her composure and returned her focus to the specialty garment on the hanger.

When Lorren saw it, she gasped.

Resting on the padded hanger was a sheer pink nightie trimmed in fluffy pink faux fur. A tiny pair of matching panties completed the outfit. The delicate, see-through material sent a delicious shiver deep between Lorren's legs.

"That's gorgeous," Lorren whispered.

"Try it on," Miss Lila smiled.

Lorren slipped the silky nightie over her head and it fluttered into place. The soft pink shade made her soft brown skin gleam. Her thick nipples were deliciously visible through the thin fabric. Her slim waist and rounded hips looked lovely in the delicate pink shade. The faux fur tickled her heated skin and she giggled.

Lorren looked at herself in the mirror and smiled. She looked angelic. Tears welled up in her eyes.

"You look gorgeous, hon," Miss Lila said. "Now, what about the panties?"

Lorren looked at her in surprise. "I can't try those on too, can I? I mean—"

"Of course you can. You must." Miss Lila unclipped them from the hanger. "Here you go." Miss Lila, her eyes fixed on the bare skin between Lorren's legs, handed her the tiny swatch of material.

Lorren slipped the panties on and looked in the mirror. She grinned wickedly.

"Wait. I need to fit this better in the front," Miss Lila said. She turned Lorren around to face her. Miss Lila reached out and stroked Lorren's firm breasts.

A moan escaped Lorren's lips as she felt Miss Lila's hands caress her gently. Miss Lila continued squeezing and passionately kneading Lorren's hot flesh. She loved stroking Lorren's firm breasts.

Needing a taste of the delicious skin, Miss Lila lowered the nightie and bent in close to Lorren's stiff nipple. She stuck her tongue out and teased the firm peak. Lorren wriggled in her grasp. Miss Lila smelled the warm scent of Lorren's skin and blazing heat suddenly erupted in her. Unable to wait any longer, she quickly sucked the Lorren's nipple into her hot, wanting mouth.

"Oooh!" Lorren cried out. "Oh, my god!"

Miss Lila's strokes became more heated as she licked and sucked the delicate flesh. She rolled her tongue over and over Lorren's silky skin. She moved to her other breast and furiously lapped at the moist peak. Lorren, dazed with passion, grabbed Miss Lila's head and pulled it tightly to her breasts. The heat between the two women threatened to scorch them both.

"The panties need fitting, too," Miss Lila said as she sank to her knees. She licked her lips as she gazed at Lorren's soft skin. She lifted the nightie and pressed her lips against Lorren's stomach. She tongued her navel, making Lorren giggle with delight. Enjoying the warmth, Miss Lila pressed her cheek to Lorren's blazing skin. She then began to plant tiny kisses all over Lorren's tight body. She continued her delicious licking and teasing until Lorren cried out in sheer pleasure.

Growing bolder, Miss Lila hooked her fingers into the tiny panties. She looked up at Lorren. "Yes?"

"Yes," Lorren whispered.

Lorren closed her eyes as she felt the panties slide down her legs. Her body tensed in anticipation. Lorren needed release badly; her hunger for this incredibly elegant and exotic woman threatened to consume her.

Then she felt it. The hot, wet tongue licking all over her smooth mound. Lorren groaned in ecstasy. Miss Lila made long, wet strokes all over Lorren's bare, swollen lips. Lorren almost screamed at the wet, wiggling sensations.

"Oh, yes," she moaned as Miss Lila licked and kissed her wet pussy. Drowning in pleasure, she reached up and began stroking her breasts. She pinched her nipples and gasped at the electric feelings racing through her.

Miss Lila nudged Lorren's legs further apart. "You taste so good, honey," she whispered before she gripped Lorren's hips and drank deeply from Lorren's heated core.

"Oh, baby," Lorren groaned. Her head spun at the feelings rushing through her.

Miss Lila moaned as Lorren's sugary juices bathed her lips. "Give me more, Lorren."

"Oooh!" Lorren cried. "That feels so good!"

"You like that, baby?" Miss Lila teased Lorren's swollen clit until Lorren began to shake. Her head rolled from side to side and tears slipped from her eyes at the intense pleasure.

"Oh, baby, please!" Lorren's senses were on overload. She sighed and moaned as she raced closer and closer to the ultimate explosion. "Don't stop! I'm so close," she panted. White-hot liquid flowed like lava from her juicy mound.

Miss Lila tongued sharp circles all over Lorren's engorged clit.

Over and over, she sweetly teased the pink gem. Finally, she slipped her index finger deep into Lorren's wetness. "Come on, Lorren. Come for me, sweet baby!"

Lorren's body lurched, desperate to reach the final pinnacle of ecstasy. "Yes! I'm coming! Now!"

Miss Lila quickly inserted a second finger. She pushed and pushed until she reached Lorren's G-spot.

"Ahhh!" Lorren screamed as her mind shattered and exploded into a thousand crystals of light. Sweet, sticky juice flowed out of her, and Miss Lila lapped up every drop. Lorren moaned and cried out her immense joy. Miss Lila held on tight, sucking and lapping at Lorren's sweet nectar.

Lorren's moans and whimpers continued until she finally floated back to Earth. Once she regained control over herself, she looked around. She suddenly realized where she was and what had just happened.

"Oh, my god! Did I just—? In a fitting room? Oh, no!" Lorren put her head in her hands.

"Lorren? Calm down, honey." Miss Lila used her tongue and fingers to trace random circles over Lorren's velvety thighs and calves. "Relax, baby."

Miss Lila stood and embraced her. The two women shared the intimate warmth from each other's bodies. Their mutual heat comforted and nourished them both.

After a few moments, they pulled apart and Miss Lila again took Lorren's hands in hers. "First things first. Do you want to purchase the items I've shown you?"

Lorren laughed and nodded.

"Good. I'll ring everything up as you go ahead and get dressed. Just come on out when you're ready." She gently touched Lorren's cheek and smiled. Miss Lila gave her a quick wave as she left the fitting room.

A few minutes later, Lorren emerged fully clothed and holding the pink nightie set. Miss Lila wrapped it in delicate tissue paper and placed it in Lorren's bag with the other garments. Once Lorren settled her bill, Miss Lila handed her the bag.

"Thanks." Lorren grinned. "And by the way—I want you to know that you've given me myself back. And I truly appreciate it."

"My pleasure." Miss Lila winked. "And as a special gift, I tossed in a few nice pieces for you. They're on the house, of course. Maybe you'll come back and model them for me?"

Lorren blushed.

Miss Lila laughed. "In any event, my business card's in the bag. Call me anytime."

Lorren smiled and nodded. As she took her bag and walked out, she turned back to Miss Lila. "Thank you so much. For everything." Lorren winked and strolled out, swinging her bag happily.

Miss Lila smiled as she watched Lorren's tight ass swish away.

Just then, the shop's telephone rang. Miss Lila smiled as she answered. "Summer Rose Lingerie."

"Hello?" the shaky voice asked. "Is this Miss Lila?"

"Yes it is. How can I help you?"

"Well," the voice started, "I got your card from a friend. She recommended you highly. She said you could help me?"

Miss Lila beamed. "Yes, I believe I can. We here at Summer Rose Lingerie are convinced that all women are beautiful, unique, and special. So it's our pleasure to do everything we can to make sure you always get the perfect fit."

TRADITIONAL INUIT THROAT SINGING

GISELLE RENARDE

THEY'D ONLY COME FOR the soapstone carvings. Rusidan's parents liked the little blue Inuksuks and polar bears, so that's what she and Sarah bought them every Christmas. Once you find a gift that works, you stick with it. It was a kind of Trojan Horse, they figured. These little presents ingratiated Sarah more and more with Rusidan's parents. If they could fill Mom and Dad's home with signifiers of Inuit culture, maybe they would begin to appreciate this incredible Inuk who'd been living with their daughter for almost four years. It wasn't much of a plan, but it was working little by little. They were coming around. They might even like Sarah by the time she and Rusidan announced their wedding plans.

How fitting that the city's first ever *Celebration of the Arctic* festival should coincide with the first major snowfall of the year. It was one of those days when you'd normally only leave the house to do something really important, like give birth. That's if you were a city mouse like Rusidan. If you were Sarah, born and raised in the frigid North, this storm barely qualified as a flurry. There was relativity, even in the weather.

Though she'd never admit it, Sarah had been waiting with bated breath for this modest celebration of her cultural heritage. Rusidan could always tell. And still Sarah looked out at the snow-capped pines and said, "It's okay. We don't have to go. No big deal."

"No way we're missing this," Rusidan sang. "Get your boots on, Lucy! Don't you know you're in the city?"

"What?"

"Never mind." That's what happens when you spend eight hours a day in an "active lifestyle" seniors complex. Her outdated references were lost on everyone outside work. "Just get dressed. We're not going to let a little snowfall keep us home."

Sarah's hair, tied into an effortless ponytail, was the exact color of a chestnut. Her forehead rested against the kitchen cupboard as she washed up the two coffee cups and two cereal bowls from breakfast. Even gazing at the back of her lover's head, Rusidan could tell she was smiling.

"You should wear your special parka," Rusidan encouraged, opening the closet door to sort through the lost land of dry cleaning bags. The anorak was pristine white with black bands stitched with images of waterfowl across the front and around the wrists and the hood. Sarah had worn it so rarely that even the fringe of blue, red and black beads remained intact.

"I don't know. I don't want to get it dirty," Sarah objected, draining the sink and drying her hands on the premature Christmas dishtowels. "It's for special occasions."

"A Celebration of the Arctic is a special occasion," Rusidan encouraged.

"I want to save it for a special-er occasion," Sarah returned with an almost imperceptible blush. Their wedding. So she was serious about getting married in the snow . . . ?

"Well, it's not a bandage you use once and throw away. If it gets dirty, we'll have it cleaned." Rusidan held the anorak up against her lover and Sarah ran her fingers across the beaded fringe like a child tentatively plucking at guitar strings. "You should wear it."

Sarah smiled slightly, as if taken to sea by an unrelated thought. "Yeah, okay."

Never could betray her inner feelings, that girl. It kept her mysterious, sure, but it was frustrating at times. She couldn't just say, "Yeah, I'm excited about this." Of course, that's the very quality Rusidan fell in love with: the whole take-it-or-leave-it attitude. Other girls were so needy. Sarah always kept a cautious distance. Problem was, that eternal vigilance never faded away. Sarah would always be distant and, if they were going to be married, that's something Rusidan was just going to have to swallow.

They had to take the subway almost to the end of the line, but anything was better than trying to negotiate roads that wouldn't be cleared before noon. The stormy weather had subsided and the city was left with falling snow, fluffy like cotton balls. Sarah's favorite weather. Rusidan liked it, too, because Sarah did. The showing of city dwellers at the outdoor festivities was disappointing, but at least the exhibitors could find some consolation in knowing it was because of the storm. Or maybe the visitors from up North didn't realize that modest snowfall was considered a storm nearer to the 49th parallel. Maybe they figured Southern Canada just wasn't interested in their lives. Worse yet, maybe they were right.

"What should we do first?" Rusidan asked, overcompensating with enthusiasm. "It's your day!"

Sarah cracked a smile. "Let's see if they're selling *muktut*!"

"I don't know what that is."

Shaking her head, Sarah explained, "Muktut is the best treat in the world: whale blubber!"

Scrunching her nose, Rusidan replied, "Yummy . . ."

"Oh, like deep-fried chicken skin is so much better!"

Rusidan hadn't seen her lover this giddy in years. She had no idea how much Sarah missed her culture, living so far away from her family. Thank God they'd battled the snow to get here. It was definitely worth the journey. While Rusidan wandered toward the vendors, Sarah ran off to find the kind of food city folk couldn't conceive of eating.

"They didn't have muktut, so I got caribou jerky. Try some." Sarah beamed. It wasn't terrible. "Before we shop for your mom and dad's gift, we should visit the indoor pavilion. Some of the athletes getting ready for the Arctic Winter Games are in there showing off." Who outside the Arctic even knew there were Arctic Winter Games? Not Rusidan, that's for sure. "After that we can watch the throat singing."

If ever you have the opportunity to witness firsthand the magnificent spectacle that is Inuit throat singing, don't pass it by.

There is nothing on this planet so cosmically beautiful. On the outdoor stage stood two young women, nothing but a microphone between them. Gripping one another, hands on forearms, they cuddled so close together their faces nearly touched. They sang a cappella and needed no accompaniment. One began before the other, producing a breathy sound. Lower than low, like a subsonic pant, the beat of her chant pushed forward like a freight train. How could a female voice produce tones so deeply resonant?

Her partner joined in, filling the gaps. The second starter vocalized at a higher pitch, singing in fleeting, orgasmic sounds. This was like nothing ever heard in Western music. The effect was intriguing, transfixing, visceral, resonating in the core of Rusidan's being. Rhythmic vibrations rumbled her body like the bass line at a rock concert. Who'd have thought throat singing would be such a turn-on? Sexual and spiritual—a divine union. Those women must be partners, the way they focused on one another, faces so close they could kiss. They rocked one another's bodies, pushing and pulling outstretched arms along with the music. They danced to the very song they created. It was stunning. Beyond stunning. It was spellbinding.

With a burst of laughter, the joiner broke away. Her partner giggled, too, giving a playful push, as if to deny their beautiful act had ever taken place. Throat singing was pure female sensuality to Rusidan. It seemed almost tawdry that she should witness their show of intimacy. As the women came down from the stage to circulate, she asked Sarah if it was customary for women to perform this ritual act in front of other people.

"It's just a game," Sarah replied, rolling her eyes.

Rusidan was taken aback. "What do you mean?"

"Throat singing is a competition to see who can keep it going the longest," Sarah explained. "We used to play at recess, like have a bit of a tournament: two girls started out and the first one to laugh was the loser. The winner played the next girl, and it kept going until the best one beat everyone else."

Unable to conceal her disappointment, Rusidan sneered, "It's just a game? But what about . . ."

An unfamiliar voice interrupted: "Sarah! Aksunai, Sarah! Over here."

Following the ebullient greeting and Sarah's gaze over her shoulder, Rusidan turned to see one of the throat singers waving in their direction. It was the "loser," the one who'd laughed first. She was a beautiful moon-faced girl with short stylish hair, molasses-colored with golden highlights.

"You know her?" Rusidan exclaimed.

"I know them both. We grew up together."

"Why didn't you say so? Tell me, are they—" She couldn't get the question out before the throat-singing pair huddled in beside them.

"Aksutik," Sarah greeted the pair, face like a Halloween mask.

The winning singer, a tallish woman with hair in a dark ponytail, stared down at her shoes. Sarah did the same. Somebody had to compensate for her juvenile pouting. Who knows what that was about? Disturbed by the tension, Rusidan gushed, "That was incredible, what you did onstage. I was moved, truly. You have no idea."

"Thanks," bubbled the girl with the warm green eyes. "It's so great that we're getting the chance to do this. I've never been to the big city before."

Mittened hands in the pockets of her parka, Sarah's head was still lowered in a glower. Rusidan tried not to grit her teeth; bad for the enamel. Turning back to the kinder Inuk, she asked, "How are you liking the trip?"

"People get all worked up about a little bit of snow," the taller woman snapped.

The hush was deadly, so the other girl compensated with, "I like it here. There are so many people living their lives in all kinds of ways. Even though there's not much space to move around, there's mental space. There's open-mindedness. It's different where we're from, right Sarah?"

Sarah exhaled loudly through flared nostrils. Just when Rusidan was convinced her partner wasn't going to respond, she answered with a reluctant, "Yeah."

When nobody said anything, Rusidan started to ask how long the women had been performing together just as the moon-faced girl began her introductions. "This is Palluq and I'm Laura. If Sarah didn't mention it, Palluq is—"

"—a fucking cunt, is what Palluq is!" Sarah erupted, turning on her heels to stomp away through snow halfway to her knees. Of course, Rusidan's impulse was to follow, to console, but she knew from experience what that would look like. She would run after Sarah, pawing at her arm, asking what was wrong. Sarah would shift her hands away, claiming it was nothing, just leave her alone. What was the point in going after her enigmatic lover? If Sarah needed space, let Sarah have her space. Plus, sadly, she was more likely to get the inside scoop from this Laura girl than her own partner.

"What was that all about?" Rusidan asked, trying to keep her tone casual.

Even Laura said nothing.

"So . . ." Rusidan searched for an inane question to ask the performers. "Do you do this for a living, throat singing? Or is it just a hobby?"

The taller woman, Palluq, threw her head back and cackled.

"We're semiprofessional, I guess you'd say," Laura clarified.

"There ain't a hell of a lot of money in the throat-singing industry," Palluq carried on, her tone a little on the demeaning side. "It was almost a lost art. We Inuk forgot the good it did us. Now it's coming back into its own, after all that self-righteous Christian malice."

Without thinking, Rusidan set her hand to cover over the cross around her neck. Like they could even see it, buried under thermal underwear, a sweater, and a winter coat.

"She probably doesn't know about the ban," Laura said to Palluq.

"What ban?" Rusidan probed.

Flicking the cotton ball snowflakes from her hair, Laura replied, "Throat singing was banned for, like, a hundred years."

"The Christian priests murdered our culture, slaughtered everything about us that was unique. Tried to, at least," Palluq accused. Rusidan covered over her cross with both hands now.

"That's a little harsh, don't you think?" Laura tempered her singing partner.

"Don't be such a wimp," Palluq replied, a little too loudly. Meeting Rusidan's gaze for the first time—and nearly bowling her over with those intense eyes—Palluq continued, "Our people didn't have written histories. Throat singing is a part of us, a part of our history, and we were robbed of it for more than a hundred years by men who had no right. Any attempt to destroy our oral history is an attempt to obliterate us as a people. And see how good that worked? People like me and Laura are rebuilding, yeah, but it takes effort. If we weren't willing to try, fifty years from now it would be like we never existed."

Laura latched her hand around the arm of Rusidan's jacket. Beaming, the moon-faced girl rolled her eyes and said, "Don't listen to Palluq; she's an extremist. We do this because we love it." This Laura girl obviously played the softener, always trying to make her partner more palatable.

A hint of a smile broke across Palluq's lips, so that Rusidan didn't quite believe her when she said, "Not me. I'm just in it for the politics."

The tension broke like a dandelion blossom and Rusidan's lungs started taking in air again. "So, do you really hate our city so much?" she asked.

"No," Palluq replied, intonation rising then falling. "It's important for us to come all the way down here to the cities to show that, yeah, we Inuk are still here, we've held on to our culture. Sure, those bastards tried to annihilate us, but we're still here."

Rusidan wasn't sure if she was more like the bastards or the throat singers. In defensive mode, perhaps, she said, "My parents came here from Georgia when I was two." Did she expect them to realize her intent was to show that she, that her family, hadn't been the ones oppressing their people? "Georgia the country, not Georgia the state."

Laura fished for something in her pocket before asking, "Georgia . . . in Africa?"

"No, Geography Drop-Out!" Palluq teased with a playful punch to her arm. "It's near Russia. Anyway, we're back on in five, so we gotta go." Turning her gaze back, she then asked, "What did you say your name was?"

"Rusidan."

"Rusidan. Write that down, will ya, Laura?" With that, Palluq headed back to the stage without offering even the customary goodbye.

Before following her, Laura clasped Rusidan tightly by the arm. "Tell Sarah we miss her and we love her. Not just me; Palluq too, and everyone else. We hope she's having a good life way down here."

"I hope so too . . ." It was so hard to tell.

When Rusidan arrived at their front door, she could hear the hockey game right through it even before she put the key in the lock. Everything back to normal, Sarah sprawled on the couch, eyes fixed on the TV. Rusidan dropped her keys into the metal bowl in the front hall from enough of a height that they made a loud clinking noise, but Sarah didn't turn around. Opening the fridge, she peered inside, then opted instead for a cup of hot chocolate. From the kitchen, she watched her lover as the kettle reached its boiling point.

"Do you want some hot chocolate?"

Sarah held up her beer in response.

The kettle rumbled until the automatic shut-off clicked. "If that's supposed to mean 'No, thank you,' then fucking say, 'No, thank you.' What's more important, the hockey game or having a real conversation with the woman you say you want to marry? And what the fuck, Sarah? Would you like to tell me what the fuck that was all about, today? We were having a good time, you were happier than I've ever seen you, then you have to go and fucking ruin it! What the fuck?"

Sarah turned off the TV, gazing blankly at Rusidan's reflection in the black screen. Setting her beer on the side table, she glided off the couch and onto the carpet. "Come, sit."

Like her lungs were bound in plastic wrap, Rusidan dragged her heels over to the living room carpet. Sarah was going to tell her she didn't want to get married anymore. They should break up. That Palluq girl was her first love and she realized today how much she'd missed an Inuk girlfriend. Reluctantly, she sat cross-legged before her partner, but Sarah hooked her feet around her back, encouraging Rusidan to do the same.

"Were they . . . that Palluq girl . . ."

With blue light glowing in from the snow-land outside, Sarah placed her hands on Rusidan's cheeks. She kissed her lips slowly, tenderly, then kissed her nose like a playful afterthought. "Palluq's my cousin."

Fears much assuaged, Rusidan smiled broadly.

"She's the one who told my parents. She's the reason I'm an outcast."

Rusidan's smile faded and she felt somehow like she'd done something wrong. "What about Laura? She seemed really happy to see you. Oh, and she wanted me to let you know they love you and miss you and hope your life is going well."

Gaze falling to the floor, then rebounding until it met Rusidan's, Sarah replied, "That's my sister for ya. She always was the caregiver."

It wasn't wise to probe for information. Instead, Rusidan grazed Sarah's upturned wrists with her fingertips, brushing them slowly up her forearms and into her elbow pits. Sarah gasped. That was good to hear. Working up the nerve, Rusidan asked, "Will you teach me throat singing? I want to try."

Closing the gap between their bellies, Sarah offered, "We could do it the old way."

"What's the old way?"

"In the old days, the women would sing with their lips almost touching. They'd use each other's mouths as a resonator, like if you speak when you're about to drink from a glass. The sound is amplified."

Rusidan could nearly lick Sarah's lips, her mouth hovered so close by. Her lover grasped her forearms just like Laura and Palluq had done. "Wait, I don't know what to do," Rusidan preempted.

"It isn't easy," Sarah admitted. "Just follow my lead; we'll do it like a copycat game. I'll start with a sound and you just give it right back to me, but maybe on a higher vocal tone. It takes a lot of practice to get that deep resonance. Just remember it's like a repetition, but it moves fast. You sing in my gaps. Does that make sense?"

"I think so."

Barley-sweet breath filled the air as Sarah began a series of deep pants. Breathy moans filled Rusidan's awestruck mouth as she began to echo her partner. The sounds she produced were not so low, but breathy like the lead-up to an orgasm. They melted into Sarah's mouth, their singing melding to create something more powerful than music. It was prayer. It was . . .

A coughing fit seized Rusidan. Wanting to push forward, she hadn't taken in enough air. "Circular breathing," Sarah advised, petting her back until the sputtering subsided. "You have to breathe in your gaps or else you'll faint."

"Am I supposed to be saying words in your language?" Rusidan inquired.

"Doesn't matter. You can sing words or just whatever sounds come out."

"Okay, meaningless sounds it is, since I don't speak Inuktitut."

"No, not meaningless," Sarah elucidated. "The sounds you produce reflect your environment, whether they come out as birdsongs or animal howls or the murmurs of sea life deep under water. Or they could reflect children's laughter on the playground or the cacophony of the city streets. Even nonsense sounds have meaning."

Rusidan breathed deeply, ruminating on her partner's words. Who knew such insight was enclosed in the sacred temple that was Sarah? Still waters, and all that.

"Lie back for a sec," Sarah instructed with a keen glint in her eye. "No, get up on the couch. That's better." Pulling off Rusidan's cords and long underwear, Sarah sat before her, hot breath upon her lower lips. Clever little horndog! If Sarah wanted those deep moans to reverberate in Rusidan's cunt, this sure was the best way to do it. "Now you don't need to worry about losing . . ."

As Sarah approached the unfolding layers of Rusidan's pussy, she produced those sounds like the chugging of an ethereal steam train. Lips touched lips and Rusidan leapt from her skin at the sheer electricity, hovering above her body as her hands flew backwards to grasp the sofa. Her cunt filled with the vibrations of Sarah's meaningful nonwords, shivering and drooling as her core expanded like a mind in meditation. Laura had said the space of the city wasn't a landscape, but a mindscape. This communion with the cunt was an element of the life Sarah couldn't lead back home.

To the deep moaning pants, Rusidan replied with soft puffs of air. She sang in Sarah's gaps. As the pace of her lover's vibrating syllables increased, so did the swirling pleasure against Rusidan's swollen lips. Her cunt filled with trembling pulsations, a seashell imparting the secrets of its source. It was a rolling feeling, a continuity, like being pulled in a cart over a series of small hills, bouncing a little when you hit the bottom, then working back up again, falling again. Yes, it was a rising and a falling, singing and gasping, giving and taking, feeling and sensing.

Rusidan grasped for Sarah's hair, completing the trembling circle of sound emanating from her partner's core, rising up through her own. Her legs were shaking now, her feet quivering uncontrollably. Sarah's throat singing was lost in Rusidan's body, a feeling more than a sound. The music was so deep, so resonant, it was like another voice coming through Sarah, coming through Rusidan. It was a spirit voice and, though it spoke in a whisper, it was all she could hear.

Filled with glowing, pulsating warmth, Rusidan rubbed her swollen clit against Sarah's nose, its puffs of warm air no match for the heat of her cunt. Vibrations were everywhere, taking over her body right to her fingertips as she struggled to press her pussy lips into her lover's willing face. Sarah sang harder, moaning sympathetically, but Rusidan was the first to break. She lost the game with an explosion of celestial laughter, the happy Buddha.

When Sarah settled her cheek against Rusidan's bare thigh, she revealed what the spirit voice had whispered. "We should get married at Christmas."

The simple ceremony took place in the snow. There were no great surprises. They knew very well which of the invited guests would choose to attend and which would not. The effort was made to reach out, and that's the best they could do. Winter sun sparkled against the crystalline blanket of white embracing their wonderland. Rusidan chose a long red jacket with matching 1920s-style cloche hat, while Sarah wore her special parka. Their aisle was a tree-lined path, and they walked it to the mesmerizing music of Laura and Palluq's traditional Inuit throat singing.

TIGHT SWEATER

JACQUELINE APPLEBEE

I RECEIVED THE PARTY INVITE late; my useless postman always seemed to mix up my mail with Abena's, the woman who lived in the flat upstairs. I'd lost count of all the times that she'd handed me my misdirected catalogs for sex toys, or my subscription to *Slick Chicks* quarterly lesbian magazine.

"Hi, Lucy. Anything nice?" Abena asked me expectantly, with the slight lilt of her Nigerian accent catching my ears. She handed over the thin pink envelope, and smiled wide.

I had a more than sneaking suspicion that she was secretly paying the postman to let her have my stuff first, so she could nose about in my naughty affairs. It's not that I'm ashamed or anything, but she looked way too turned on that evening when she gave me my mail. Abena had a habit of hopping about from foot to foot when she was excited, with her dark, almost black eyes opening wide. She was a cute woman, but I didn't want to get involved with anyone in the same building—if we fell out, it would be hell, I was sure of it.

I made an excuse, and rushed back indoors. The letter was from my dear friend, Robin, who lived outside London in the quaint town of St. Albans. I read the card, which contained an invitation to his birthday party. The party would have a fancy dress theme—it was going to be based on an American 1950s drive-in. Robin promised popcorn, burgers, and a big screen set up in his garden. There would also be a showing of his boyfriend, Jake's, favorite porno movie to round it all off. Robin had a real love of the whole retro scene, and his lovely home was full of kitsch—make that garish memorabilia from the 1950s through to the 1970s.

There was a problem, though: I only had a day to weasel out of work, get an outfit organized, and make my way to Robin's home. I wasn't sure if I could manage it.

I frantically pulled out every single item in my wardrobe, my panic growing as the evening hours slipped by. The small mountain of clothes on my bedroom floor was a testimony of how I could never turn down a clothing bargain, and how I still had nothing suitable to wear. I was getting desperate—it was almost eleven at night and I still had no outfit.

I collapsed dramatically onto the heap of clothing, laying down my weary head on the pile. That's when I spotted a half-hidden sweater; a soft-as-butter, creamy white item that I hadn't worn in years. I held up the fluffy article and realized why—it was several sizes too small for me, and the last time I had worn it, I'd almost garroted myself. It had been a snip at half the price on the tag, and I remembered how sexy I'd felt, just brushing it against my face, when I'd bought it at Wembley Market.

My mind conjured up an image; I knew this lovely sweater, matched with a few choice accessories, would be just great for the party. I swiftly massacred a pair of my old torn blue jeans, ruthlessly shearing off the legs at the knees. I put on a firm control bra that was guaranteed to make my usually modest boobs stick out like Cold War missiles, and then came the all-important tight sweater.

Oh god! I just about managed to get the thing over my head, without tearing out my blonde hair by the roots. I slowly pushed my arms through the long sleeves with painful effort. As I reached to pull the rest of the sweater down over my breasts, my fingers ached with the exertion of yanking the material down lower. It seemed to take forever to get the bloody sweater on, and I swore at the blasted thing, jumping up and down as it moved an inch at a time.

I could hardly breathe—didn't dare exhale, as I thought I might rupture something, but I finally had it on. I inched myself carefully to my full-length mirror and admired the view. I looked like a camp poster girl. I smiled widely, happy that I managed to pull the whole outfit off. I was ready for the party and I was sure that I'd have a great time, dancing the night away. I tried an experimental wiggle, giggling at the sight of me playing dress-up like a silly little girl.

Now all I had to do was pack my overnight bag, get some sleep, and in the morning—actually make that the afternoon—I could catch a train from London Bridge station straight to the town of St. Albans.

I stooped awkwardly, trying to pick up my remaining clothes off the floor, but that damn sweater was so constricting, I could hardly bend over. It was definitely time to take it off before I damaged it, or it damaged me.

I tried shouldering myself out of the sleeves first, but they just wouldn't budge. I blew out a puff of frustration, and tried lifting the horrid sweater off, rolling the lower part painfully up over my bra. I managed a few inches, scratching my own skin, as I rolled the tight material over the rounded slope of one of my tits. The scary sweater bunched up beneath my armpits in a tight, unyielding hold, and that was as far as it went. The restraining material held me incredibly rigid, lifting my arms up awkwardly with growing pain. I tried to shift the vile sweater further, but no such luck. I was well and truly stuck.

I must have stood in the middle of my bedroom, panicking and making small desperate noises for more than ten minutes. I realized that I was starting to perspire. The deceptively fluffy material slashed into my sore flesh with every movement, until the painful ache around the top of my chest grew so much that I thought that I was going to cry. I knew that I would have to get some help. I gazed up at the ceiling with trepidation.

Abena opened the door to her upstairs flat, and she gawped at me with a mixture of extreme shock and straight-up-and-down lust. She looked like she was getting ready for an evening in, wearing only an oversized blue T-shirt that barely covered her wide round backside.

"Come in, Lucy." She hurried me into her warm lounge, and stood back, drinking in the sight of me in my pathetic attire.

"It's so tight," I moaned, my words catching in my throat.

"How on earth did you do that?" She sounded exasperated, but still let out a stifled laugh. "I'd offer you a drink, but I don't think that iced tea would be any good right now," she said, flicking her head to a table near the wall. I spied a small jug of gorgeous amber liquid that looked so very refreshing, with plenty of ice cubes bobbing about like little icebergs. My throat began to ache with dryness, and I realized suddenly that I was desperate for a drink. I turned back to Abena, and she was staring straight at me.

"You've gotta help me, Abena," I sobbed. I was upset at how stupid I must have looked. The searing pain from the awful sweater cut into my ribs, pushing at my lungs so that I couldn't even speak above a whisper.

"Of course, but . . ." She gave me a meaningful look.

"But what?" I squeaked, squirming against my bonds.

"You were always too busy before," she said, having the decency to look a bit hurt.

"I'm sorry," I whined, but it was true; I had ignored her when I should have been more neighborly. I just hoped that she wouldn't hold a grudge.

"Yeah, well, you do look sorry now," she said with a naughty smirk, licking her lips slowly. She scooted to the table and poured out some iced tea. She raised the glass to my lips and I tried to drink. The tea was tart, cold, and refreshing—I started to feel a little energy coming back to me, and I felt momentarily better.

"Thank you, Abena," I said, and tried to smile, but it must have come out as a grimace. She put the glass down, and advanced on me. Abena's congenial face was gone—now she looked like a ravenous horny woman on the prowl for fresh meat. I suddenly felt like a trussed turkey, ready for the dinner table. I cowered away from her.

Abena said nothing as she yanked and tugged at the rotten sweater, jerking me around like a little rag doll. I had never realized just how well-built she was; her efforts almost made me stumble. Each time it felt like I was going to fall from one of her rough movements, she held me up in a strong grip, taking the opportunity to stroke and manhandle my burning skin. She pushed me up against the wall, and pulled the collar of the dreadful sweater over my head, blinding me with the soft opaque fabric. I could still breathe, but everything became suddenly muffled. Without that crazy horny woman in sight, my mind began to spiral, imagining Abena with a butcher's knife, or a length of corded rope in her hands.

"This is never going to come off, is it?" I whispered, trying to stay calm, but it was hard; my arm muscles were aching, and every movement was frustrated by the soft, knitted restraint that surrounded me.

"It's tight, but I love a good struggle," she growled against my ear. My knees went weak; I could practically feel the vibrations from her low voice, as it traveled right down my spine and right up my ass.

I shook as Abena tugged at the fastening of my bra. In moments my breasts were partially freed from their fetters, bobbing out from beneath the rolled up band of the tight sweater. I felt incredibly exposed, incredibly aroused, and knew my nipples were standing up like stiff little buttons.

"Lucy," Abena murmured against one breast. She swiped her wet tongue over it once, making me shiver with longing. "You're so beautiful. Your tits are just great."

Oh, god, let her suck it! Sweet words don't mean shit to me. We can do this, fall out, and I would never complain. There are more important things in life than getting on with the neighbors.

Abena dragged a short fingernail over my damp cleavage. I groaned out loud through the smothering weave of the dangerous sweater, shaking, but wanting more.

"Abena." It was all I could say—I couldn't form a more coherent sentence. I struggled against the binding fabric, even as I wanted to be held. I needed, wanted, and craved this.

"Say it again," her voice sounded the way I felt—weak, needy, and desperate.

"Abena," I purred, using what little strength I had left to push her name out through my dry lips. I shivered, plastering myself against her, against the cotton of the T-shirt that she wore. "Abena, please," I begged, closing my eyes so she wouldn't see how depraved I had become.

Suddenly I jumped and shrieked with surprise as something freezing cold was placed on my belly. I worked out that it must be one of the ice cubes from the tea, when I felt an arctic slide of water dribble down to the fly of my jeans. She rubbed the frozen nugget over my skin, and the cold burned me, making my nerves sing out with shock. My sore muscles ached and pulsed towards her. She swept the ice further up, to the underside of my breasts, and I sucked in as much air as I could, wriggling away, trying not to move, wanting this so much. She kept up this sweet agony for an age, and I was wet and hot and frozen all at the same time—making incoherent sounds, bound and wild in a single moment. I felt as if one more touch would make me explode where I stood. I never wanted this to end.

The next time I felt the ice, it wasn't against my belly. Abena unzipped my jeans, and tugged them down around my knees. I knew what was coming next—there was no denying it, and no way I could pass this one off as neighborly concern. My thoughts were interrupted as the ice touched my inner thigh. I flushed even hotter as the cold ice fairly evaporated against my skin.

"Tell me to stop anytime," Abena whispered.

"Don't," I gasped as the next piece of ice brushed against my labia. "Don't stop."

Abena chuckled, and at the same moment, she slipped another chunk of ice into my folds—it was gone within seconds; the trickle of cold water was the only evidence of what she had done. Abena spread me wider, and ran a larger piece of ice all over my cunt. It felt incredible. I could see stars as it touched my clit, and Abena held it there as I felt myself pulse and grow beneath the ice. Abena bent down and sucked at my cunt—the contrast between my arctic body and her hot mouth was out of this world. I arched up against her as she sucked harder, and then I came, cocooned within my magical sweater—my grunts swallowed by the cloth. I dragged in a lungful of air as I came down from my high, but then I yelped as Abena pushed another piece of ice right inside me. I throbbed around the melting ice, sighing as the coolness soothed me, if only for a moment.

"Sweet baby," she breathed against the cloth that covered my bound face, surprising me with the gentleness in her voice. And then she stepped away, and I was left reeling.

I could just about see the shadowy outline of Abena's form as she pulled off her T-shirt, and approached me once more. I could feel her naked heat, sweaty and smooth against my sticky belly, writhing against my exposed skin. She ran her firm hands over me, making me pant like crazy. Abena wrenched my still-bound arms over my head, making me reach up onto tiptoes with painful delight. I smelt my own body—my fragrance of soap, sweat, and wild, crazy sex. Abena pulled repeatedly at the cuffs of that sweet, lovely sweater, making my breasts wobble and bounce vigorously, before abruptly letting me go. I grunted and swore beneath my hood of cloth, mouthing against the soft fabric, trying to find purchase on any bit of Abena that I could.

I stopped my attempts suddenly as she then proceeded to pull at the fabric around my head, with firm, slow movements. The menacing sweater pressed precariously tight against my throat, making my breathing falter for a split second, and then, with blessed relief, the front of the evil sweater popped off, and I collapsed against her, gasping for fresh air.

My arms were still bound and burning from the constricting sweater, but I could breathe and I could kiss. We became locked in a half embrace in moments, with Abena exploring my mouth with her hungry lips and tongue. I was just as desperate as I had been when fully restrained, and all the pent-up desire came tumbling out of me. I backed her away from the wall and to a sofa that I spied near the windows.

Now I have to be honest with you: I could have made it out of the tight sweater from that point on, but in all truth, I just didn't want to. The feeling of being held, restrained, and at another's mercy was giving me the biggest rush of my life. Everything seemed brighter, every sound was crystal clear, and each touch to my skin was electric.

Abena and I toppled backwards onto the sofa messily. I looped my bound arms over her head, and straddled the smiling woman, grinding my hips against her beautiful body. Abena was shades of dark plum, bitter chocolate, and it was all topped off with a delightful sheen of sweat that almost glittered before my eyes.

Abena soon had my jeans completely off, shuffling them from me in a feat of contortion and then, with a final painful tearing yank, the best sweater in the whole wide world flew from me, landing in a sweaty, distorted heap on the floor.

I learned what a giving and generous neighbor Abena was that night—I also learnt that I had been mean and horrible for being suspicious of her. I was crazy to have not made a move sooner. I came three more times that night, writhing beneath her tongue, jerking around her strong fingers, and slip-sliding against her thick, sturdy knees. Abena had a good time, too, lost in the wild abandon of the evening. She showed me just how much she had wanted me since she had moved into the building by licking me all over, slurping and sucking at every inch of my body until I was raw, sore, and exhausted. I never thought I could ever feel as free as I had done while bound in that crazy, tight sweater. I never thought that Abena would be into kinky fun, either, but I was happy to have my assumptions knocked out of me. I mentally wrote out a shopping list in my head that included silky scarves, handcuffs, and blindfolds; I would have a repeat performance of this evening if it was the last thing I ever did.

I telephoned Robin the next afternoon, and he understood as always, although he wanted to know all the juicy details. He said that I should bring Abena with me for his next party at Christmas. It was going to be another fancy dress theme—this time it would be a punk-rock affair.

Abena chuckled when I told her and said she could think of a few things to do with safety pins. Then she gave me my mail and climbed back into bed, holding me tightly against her as we both fell asleep.

A DIFFERENT KIND OF HOUSE CALL

MADLYN MARCH

ONE DAY, MY LIFE WAS perfectly wonderful; the next, a strange woman's hand was up my girlfriend's pussy. I didn't ask for an explanation. What kind could there be? She was in there looking for car keys?

When I got over the shock, I realized that hand belonged to the unfortunately pseudonymed Anita Fok, star of *Horny Hospital*. Anita played a doctor who cured people by giving them orgasms. Her waiting room was always crowded with eager patients, as you might imagine.

"Ungh!" Lucy cried. "Can you—"

The good doctor knew just what Lucy needed—mouth-to-clit resuscitation. She pushed Lucy's legs back and slurped noisily.

"Oh, that's it, Anita. I'm coming."

Anita grabbed Lucy by the waist; Lucy locked her legs around Anita's neck. Meanwhile, my teeth clenched; my heart sped up; and my hands balled into fists. I was furious; I wanted to yell, but I knew Lucy and Anita wouldn't listen. They were too deep into The Sex Zone. I thought about leaving, but couldn't bear to do so. Somehow, it felt less like cheating if I was there to watch it.

Lucy scrunched up her face, moaned some more, and pumped her sexy hips against Anita's silicone-filled lips.

"Uuugggh! Ugggghh!" she cried, her thighs shaking. "Oh, my god! That feels so good! Yes! Just a little faster with your tongue. Right there on my clit. Oh, god, that's the spot. I'm getting so wet. Oh yes, Anita! Oh, my god! Oh, my god!"

I thought that would be it, but Lucy's pussy was like Chinese food, in the sense that Anita immediately demanded seconds.

"No," Lucy protested. "I can't." She tried pushing Anita's head away, but that only made Anita want it more. Anita went faster this time, using a finger to pump Lucy's hole while sucking on her clit.

After she came, Lucy looked up at me. I didn't know what to say to her and she didn't know what to say to me.

Truth be told, I wasn't too surprised. I knew one of these days Lucy would cheat on me—I just didn't think it would happen on my birthday.

A few months ago, Lucy and I were watching this particularly hot episode of *The L Word*. As soon as I shut off the TV, Lucy lifted her knees up to her chest.

"Need me to spot you for sit-ups?" I asked.

Lucy frowned.

"OK, OK," I said, not wanting to be a poor sport. We'd been going out for months now and Lucy had been very patient with me, sexually speaking.

I leaned my head down until my lips were touching her mound. I licked for a few seconds before jumping up abruptly.

"What's the matter?" Lucy asked, as I spit pubic hair onto the mattress.

"I just can't."

"All right. Look, I don't want to force you. Why don't I do you instead?"

"No." If she did me, I'd have to reciprocate, somewhere down the line. I just wanted to forget the whole thing and move on to something else.

But Lucy wasn't ready to move on. She kissed her way up my thighs. She breathed heavily on my pubic hair, and finally deposited a wiggly tongue on my engorged clit.

"No!" I said again.

"Why?"

"I told you: I just can't." I couldn't tell her the truth, which was that I was grossed out by the whole affair. I didn't want to go down on her and I couldn't imagine why she wanted to go down on me. To put your mouth where a person pees? Where a woman menstruates? Who decided that was fun? John Waters? And why did you even need to do it when a hand could do the same job in a much more civilized manner?

And then there was the other factor. To open myself up like that meant I was also opening my heart. It meant that I was making a serious commitment. I loved Lucy, but I wasn't sure I could be that kind of girlfriend. I had just come out. The whole thing was still so new. I didn't quite have my bearings yet. And the way things were going—with my mother *still* not talking to me because I refused to date her friends' sons—I wasn't sure I was ever going to be OK with this whole lesbian deal.

I began to cry. Lucy patted me on the back and assured me it wasn't that important. Of course, she was lying. Oral sex is only the most important thing in the world to a dyke. It's right up there with cats, knitting, and The Indigo Girls. Only I was the odd lesbian who didn't like it, or any of those things, for that matter. Give me dogs, rug hooking, and The Pet Shop Boys any day.

"Do you want to talk about it?" Lucy asked.

I shook my head no.

So, I guess, in the end, I got what I deserved. If I wasn't willing to be a full sexual partner for Lucy, she had the right to fuck someone else.

"Why do you look so upset?" Lucy asked.

"Why am I upset? You're cheating on me!"

"Oh, my God. Is that what you think?"

"Well, what the hell should I be thinking?"

"No, no. You've got it all wrong. It's for your birthday. A threesome!" She jumped up and down. "We were going to wait for you, but *somebody* got a little restless."

Anita looked down at the floor.

"Really?" I asked. "You're not cheating?"

"No. Why would I do that? I love you. I just wanted to add some excitement to our sex life."

"Well, I guess that's a nice idea, but I don't think I'm ready."

Lucy looked at Anita. "Can you please go into the bedroom?"

"Yes, Mistress Lucy," Anita said, tonelessly. "I am your humble servant and your loyal—"

"Later," Lucy whispered.

"But you said I'd get to act!" Anita stomped on the ground for dramatic effect, something I'm sure they taught her at Porn Actors' School.

"Go!"

Anita pouted but walked up the staircase. "Put on some panties if you're going to sit on our red chair. We just bought that," I said.

"Look, hon," Lucy said when Anita was gone. "I know this wasn't one of your fantasies, but I think it might help bring us closer together. Maybe make you less inhibited. I thought if you saw Anita and me going at it, you'd feel a little less self-conscious, a little more adventurous, and maybe want to join in. There's so much I want to do with you. Not just oral, but also S&M."

S&M.

I remembered the one time we'd messed around with that. My bare ass in Lucy's face. That scary feeling of being vulnerable. I pulled my pants up right away, not even giving Lucy the chance to touch me.

"So, can we go upstairs?" Lucy asked.

She looked so beautiful standing there, the light from the windows illuminating her alabaster skin and long blond hair. Her hopeful smile. Her pleading eyes. How could I turn her down? Did I really want to blow our relationship by not blowing her?

"All right," I said.

She smiled and we went upstairs. My heart was pounding. I'd never had group sex before. And to have to do the thing I felt most self-conscious about while someone else was watching? This was going to be awful. Yet I had to try, if I didn't want to lose Lucy.

"Are we all good, ladies?" Anita asked, lounging on the red chair, completely naked, of course. I sighed, knowing I would be throwing out that chair just as soon as she was gone.

"You do this for a living?" I asked, getting undressed.

"Yep. It's on my Web site. Under miscellaneous. That's how Lucy found me."

"Olivia loves your films, by the way," Lucy said.

"I do not!"

"Oh, please!" Lucy said. "I saw you rubbing one out last week to *ICU: Intensive Cunnilingus Unit*."

I blushed and put my head under the pillow. Anita lifted the pillow off me.

"Don't be embarrassed. I love meeting fans. Come here. I got really horny waiting for you." She pulled my hand to her cunt, all soft and slippery. I whimpered as she raced my finger up and down her hot little slit.

"W-w-what would you like me to do?" I asked.

Anita smiled at my nervousness. "Fist me."

"Oh, no. That's Lucy's department," I said, pulling my hand free.

"No it's not," Lucy said.

"I *can't* do that."

"Why not?"

"I could hurt her. Look at my nails." As a dyed-in-the-flannel butch, I usually never get my nails done, but my mother, in yet another effort to "make me straight," had given me a gift certificate, and I hate to let a thing like that go to waste. I felt like calling Mom up and thanking her for giving me such an easy out from fisting a gay porn star, but somehow I didn't think she'd approve.

"Fine, fine. Just watch me," Lucy said. So I watched, in amazement, as Lucy filled Anita's glistening pussy with her right hand. She started with just a few fingers and a lot of lube, slowly stretching the hole out. Then she began punching her pussy, like it was a boxing opponent. Anita screamed and I worried she was being hurt, but the look on her face told me otherwise. Anita was being punched, but she was still the winner.

As for myself, I could hold back no longer. I took off my own pants, lay down next to the two of them, and began masturbating. It was actually kind of nice, even liberating, to touch my cunt in public—though the two of them were far too distracted to notice me. A slight breeze came in from the window, cooling my cunt and taking the edge off my need.

But the need soon came back, multiplied by a thousand. I grabbed the newly bought vibrator on the side of the bed and slid it into myself, pushing the switch up to high. In seconds my pussy was being assaulted by the most intense vibrations I'd ever known. I moaned in pleasure and frustration, waiting for my orgasm to overtake me. Lucy and Anita stopped what they were doing and sucked my nipples, trying—I thought—to help me reach the Promised Land.

And then all of a sudden, the vibrator stopped.

Lucy had managed to reach down and shut it off. "I didn't say you could come," she announced.

"I didn't realize I had to check in with you first."

"Don't be funny," she said and began licking my left ankle. Then Anita began doing the same thing to my right one. Soon both of them were licking up my thighs.

And that's when I realized it. They both planned to go down on me at once.

I got up. I couldn't handle even one woman going down on me. No way could I handle two.

"You know, ladies, I really don't think I can do this. Why don't we just take a rain check?"

"Get the handcuffs out, Anita."

"No. Please, Lucy. I'm not ready for that."

"Olivia, do you remember the time you took me swimming?"

"Yeah."

"And do you remember how I clung to the edge and how I wouldn't jump in, even though it was the shallow end?"

"Yeah."

"And what did you do?"

"I pushed you."

"OK. Now I'm pushing you."

I sighed.

She put a hand on my shoulder. "Olivia, we deserve to have a spicier sex life. There's more to sex than just hand jobs and making out. You can't keep being so scared like this."

Anita came back with the handcuffs.

I watched my hands shake as they were attached to the bed. I began to worry. What if they lost the key? I envisioned a late-night call to a laughing locksmith.

But then another thought flew through my brain: I was completely immobilized, and at the mercy of two very horny lesbians.

Lucy bent down and put her mouth on me. Though I wanted her to go down on me, I still worried she would be repulsed by my taste, my smell.

I needn't have been concerned. "I could eat you for days,"

Lucy whispered and I could tell she really meant it. I tasted good because I was her girlfriend. She wanted to do this for me because it gave her pleasure to make me happy.

And, Christ, did it feel better than a hand job—more warm, more intimate, more intense.

I forgot about my self-consciousness and began to enjoy it. Lucy stopped when she sensed I was about to come. She kissed me, and I tasted myself on her. I was quite delicious, if I do say so myself. But even more important, this liquid was evidence that I was sexual, that I was a woman, that I was in love and loved. How could I have ever been ashamed of it?

I was so happy I wanted to cry. Lucy looked a little teary-eyed as well.

I wanted to stop and talk to her, tell her how stupid I'd been and how sorry I was now, for having denied her this, for having denied us both.

"Lucy—"

But before I could finish, Lucy went back down on me. A few minutes later, Anita joined in, and that's when things got really interesting. Anita licked to the right of my clit, Lucy to the left. But neither of them would lick my clit itself. I tried to push the cuffs off, but it was hopeless. I was stuck.

Lucy looked up. "Are we not doing a good enough job?" she asked, all fake innocence.

"I think she wants us to suck her clit," Anita said. "Do you want us to suck your clit, Olivia? Do you need a good clit-sucking? I'll tell you something. A good clit-sucking is the best thing in the world, especially when you're dying to come. And I bet it wouldn't even take that many licks to get you there. A few quick flicks of my nice, soft tongue."

I heard myself moan.

"Oh, she wants it real bad," Anita needlessly commented.

Then I felt it: one solitary lick, right in the center of my cunt, courtesy of Lucy.

"Oh yes, Lucy, god, yes. Please, more."

Lucy smiled but did not lick again.

"How do you feel?" she asked, smiling triumphantly.

"How do you *fucking* think I feel?" I asked, scowling at her.

She looked taken aback. "I know it's a little uncomfortable, but—"

"It's not just a little uncomfortable. I'm going out of my mind here, Luce. Finish me off. *Please*."

"Soon."

I groaned.

"Come on; it's kind of nice, isn't it? Not to be in control of your own orgasm?"

Lucy licked my clit again and I had to admit she was right. It did feel more exciting to be in handcuffs like this, to not be in control. Exciting, but damn frustrating.

"Oh, this is no good at all," Lucy announced. "You're dripping on my mouth. Definitely a no-no."

"That's ridiculous. I can't control what my cunt—"

Lucy gave me a look that screamed *Get with the program*.

"Oh, that's right; I am dripping. I've been a very bad girl. I guess this means you'll be punishing me," I said, in a bored tone of voice. Why did Lucy have to be this weird, this kinky? Why couldn't we just fuck like everyone else? More importantly, why couldn't we go back to her going down on me?

Lucy took me out of the handcuffs, but only to turn me around and handcuff me again. Then she pulled down my pants. I was glad my face was in the pillow because I was blushing to beat the band.

Lucy hit me with a whip. It hurt like a motherfucker. "Lucy, I—"

Lucy wrapped a belt around my mouth. She didn't care what I had to say. She whipped me again and I felt another painful, burning sensation on my butt. The burning got hotter and hotter with each hit, matching the warmth in my pussy. I would have thought the pain would blot out the pleasure, but the whipping just made me hornier. My ass was getting all the attention my pussy craved. It was driving me insane, but in the very best way.

That was when I gave up control, gave myself to Lucy. She would do what she wanted. I was hers and hers alone.

And, of course, just as I was giving up control and enjoying myself, Lucy stopped hitting me.

She took the cuffs off and turned me back over to face her and Anita, who had some odd little contraption on her tongue.

"What is that?" I asked.

"You'll see." Anita knelt down beneath my legs and placed her tongue on my clit. I was about to complain: I'd wanted Lucy to get me off. But immediately I felt such a strong vibration in my cunt, I couldn't say a damn thing. Anita kept her tongue on me for a few minutes, then withdrew.

My dignity took a suicide leap out the window.

"Anita, please, please come back. Just a little while longer and I'll—"

"And you'll come. Yes, I know."

Anita cuffed me again and walked out of the room with Lucy.

I moaned loudly, banged my head against the wall—literally. They didn't care. They were planning to make me suffer for God knows how long.

Finally, I'd just had it. "Lucy, please. I can't take any more!" I yelled.

Lucy came in. She had a worried look on her face. She seemed to know I'd hit my breaking point. She asked Anita to leave.

"I guess we went a little too far, huh? But I was so excited for you. For us. I think we really made a breakthrough.

"Yes, a breakthrough," I said, and I could barely get that much out. Lucy had gone back to going down on me.

And this time there was no teasing. Lucy licked and licked and licked, right where I needed it the most. And then it happened. The orgasm exploded out of me like a massive volcano, leaving me a sweating, crying mess.

"Oh, Lucy," I said. "I love you so much."

I got up from the bed.

"Where are you going?" she asked.

"I'm going to cut my nails. I don't want to hurt you."

THURSDAY NIGHTS IN SOHO

CLAIRE MARTIN

IT WAS NEARLY NINE O'CLOCK before Ryan emerged from her City office building and began hunting for a cab. As was usually the case, work had kept her longer than she intended and now she would be late meeting her friend Val in Soho at the bar that had a Thursday Lesbian Night. She'd hoped to be able to stop at her flat to change clothes, feeling her chance of hooking up with someone was greater in her hot casual rather than tailored professional look. And hooking up was entirely the goal of these once-a month-meetings with Val.

A black cab pulled over and Ryan stared out the window at the London streets as they crawled through traffic. After transferring from New York and living in London for four years, the magic had worn off a bit, but she still loved the city. It was entirely cosmopolitan, yet comfortable and tradition bound at the same time. She'd been fortunate to make friends with Val early on, and from there she developed a network of friends, most of them British, most of them lesbians. But no girlfriend had materialized from that ever-expanding network of people. To satisfy her need for sex, Ryan went for the least involving encounters she could find and concentrated on her career.

Ryan paid off her cab and dashed across Old Compton Street to the entrance of The Wine Bin Soho. As she was checking her coat at the front she heard Val hail her from the bar and she hurried over to join her.

"God, I'm so sorry I'm late. Usual reasons, I'm afraid."

"Of course, not to worry. I was about to call you on your mobile and tell you not to bother coming. It's bloody dull as dust in here." Val poured Ryan a glass of wine from the open bottle before her.

Ryan took a sip as she perused the room. The wine bar was one large room decorated in Euro blond wood and chrome, with booths along one wall, a long bar along the opposite wall, and tall bar tables and stools placed in the space between. The booths were all full, but the bar and the tables were only half occupied. A much darker back room housed the sound system and dance floor, with the DJ scheduled to start at 10:00.

"Well, I suppose it's early yet," Ryan said, "but you're right about the company. It's everyone we see each time we come here."

"I know. I'm going to die of boredom. I'll keel over right here at the bar, done in by ennui." Val lit a cigarette in exaggerated exasperation, and turned once more to observe the floor. "Oh, bloody hell, there's that Sandy whatsits, the one from last month." Val twirled back to face the bar again.

Ryan tried not to laugh as she saw a woman get off her bar stool and make her way toward them. "Incoming at twelve o'clock high," she said, poking Val in the shoulder. "You're going to have to fight your way out."

Sandy marched up to Val and spun her bar stool around so that Val faced her, wine glass at her lips. Val lowered her glass and smiled. "Sandy, how nice to see you."

"Oh, piss off, Val. I think your failure to return three phone calls shows just how glad you are to see me." Val leaned back a bit from the smell of alcohol on Sandy's breath.

"Well, I don't even know how you got my phone number. And anyway, I was out of town. And my mother was sick."

"Are you done?" Sandy asked.

"Oh, yes."

"Good. 'Cause I don't give a shit anyway. You're a total cad and I don't want to waste my time with you. I'm here to ask your friend if she wants to have a dance."

Val made a choking sound as Ryan turned slowly in her chair to face Sandy. "Are you talking about me?" Ryan asked. "I just sat down, and I don't think they're even playing music yet."

"Well, later then. Come find me." Sandy placed her hand on Ryan's arm and started to move away.

Ryan held Sandy's hand and said, "You should know that I'm a total cad as well. I don't think you'll want to waste your time with me, either."

"We'll see. Look me up later." Sandy walked away and rejoined her friends.

Ryan stared after her and then looked at Val, who was pouring more wine into their glasses. "You know, it's gotten so we're really not much better than men. We're kind of pathetic."

"What do you mean?" Val asked.

"Well, we come here once a month on Lesbian Night with pretty much the sole intention of getting laid. I think we can safely say that with a few notable exceptions, most of the lesbians are here with the sole intention of meeting someone, and I don't mean just to get laid. They want to fall in love. So in order to get laid we do exactly what men do, which is to give the women we're seducing the impression that there's some meaning to the encounter beyond the few hours we spend with them. They are more likely to come across if they think we are sincere in this way."

"Well, I can hardly deny it," Val said. "It's a tried-and-true technique."

"We've also developed an attitude that somehow ridicules the very women who have believed our lies, which is not only cruel but doesn't make a whole lot of sense. We are truly fucked up."

Val was quiet for a minute. "You're just realizing this now?"

"What, have you always known you're a bastard?"

"Yes, but it was much easier to live with when it wasn't articulated in such a brutally frank manner." Val turned back to the bar and hunched over her glass. "It's just that I'm not ready to fall in love. I like sleeping with lots of different women. If there were more dykes like us it would be so much easier. Everybody plays, no one gets hurt."

"I'm not sure populating the world with more dykes like us would be a good idea for anyone."

They sat morosely for awhile, Val facing the bar, Ryan watching the room. As they drank and brooded, the music finally started up. The dark room in back was now faintly illuminated by the colored lights around the DJ booth and the disco ball hanging from the ceiling. As women started to rise and make their way over to dance, the lights in the main room were lowered.

"That helps," observed Val. "That and another bottle of wine and I might start liking myself again, no thanks to you."

Ryan wasn't listening to Val as she watched the front door open and two women enter. They were both clad in long wool coats which they left at the coat check and as they started to make their way across the room Ryan gave Val a tap on her shoulder. "Hold on. The evening might be salvageable."

Val looked over as the two women took over an abandoned booth. They were roughly Val and Ryan's ages, dressed smartly in the same kind of professional lesbian wear that Val and Ryan wore. One of them, a tall beauty with auburn hair, approached the bar and placed their order. Her companion stayed behind and used a hand mirror to freshen up her makeup. She was lovely as well, with a short, layered cut to her blonde hair. Val and Ryan looked at each other.

"What do you think?" asked Ryan. "Friends or lovers?"

"I'm thinking friends. But we need to observe a bit more, I feel. It's just embarrassing if you get that wrong."

"Agreed." They continued their conversation as they stole glances at the booth, debating who would go for the blonde, who for the auburn-haired woman. For Ryan there was no question who she preferred. She couldn't take her eyes off the woman now returning from the bar with drinks in hand.

Miranda placed the wine and glasses onto the table and settled herself across from Diane. "Anything happening yet?"

"Oh, yes. Two live ones over there at the bar. They're trying to pretend that they're not looking at us."

"And they're also debating whether we're friends or lovers and if we're friends, who is going to go off with whom." Miranda pushed a full glass of wine over to her colleague.

"Yes, I'm sure you're right." Diane put her mirror away and gave Miranda a brilliant smile. "I'd love to play around and confuse the hell out of them before reeling them in, but I'm not sure I have the energy this evening."

"No, me neither. Let's let them know we're available and see how long before they come over. They look the right sort, don't you think?"

"They'll do," Diane agreed. "I don't think money's a problem."

"And they aren't half bad-looking, are they?" Miranda observed. "I'll take the dark-haired one, if you don't mind."

Ryan swept her dark hair away from her face and turned to Val again. "I'd say definitely friends. They were just looking around the bar like they were checking things out. Hey, I think they're checking us out."

"Are they still looking?"

"Yeah, and smiling, too. Let's do it. I go auburn, you go blonde."

Fifteen minutes later Ryan found herself on the dance floor with Miranda in her arms. She'd become completely intrigued by Miranda within a minute of sitting next to her in the booth. She was gorgeous and intelligent, with an easy, straightforward manner. Ryan pulled her closer as the music slowed and leaned forward to speak.

"I usually am here once a month. Have you been here before?" she asked.

"Last week was the first time."

"And what do you think?"

Miranda wrapped her hands behind Ryan's neck and smiled. "I think I'm going to enjoy myself more than I did last week."

God, I hope that means what I think it means, Ryan thought. She was starting to want Miranda badly. As they moved lightly to the music, Ryan heard herself gasp as Miranda's thigh moved between her legs.

"Felt that, did you?" Miranda smiled, and then leaned in to kiss Ryan. As the kiss deepened Ryan felt her heart accelerate and realized she was already fully aroused. She broke the kiss and looked back at Miranda.

"You don't waste time, do you?"

"No point. I think we'll get along just fine." Miranda's hand wandered down the front of Ryan's shirt, pausing to discretely pinch a nipple along the way. The sensation streaked like lightning to Ryan's clitoris and her eyes got a little wider.

"I'd say it's a sure thing," Ryan said, moving her hands lower to feel the swell of Miranda's ass.

"There's something you should know right away, though."

Oh, god. There's always something. "Okay," Ryan said. "What?"

"I'm a professional." Miranda looked into Ryan's eyes to gauge her reaction, and what she saw was the usual confusion.

"Okay. Um, I'm a professional also. Investment banking."

"You're adorable, but I'm afraid that's not what I meant. My profession's much older than yours."

A flash of disappointment hit Ryan as she realized Miranda was a prostitute. She didn't like the idea of Miranda sleeping with men, though she knew she needed to act cool about it. Maybe Miranda would find a new line of work. Or Ryan could support her. She made tons of money. And maybe she shouldn't get so ahead of herself.

"That's really interesting," Ryan said, continuing to guide Miranda in a shuffling two step. The disco ball went into action, which always seemed to have a sad and desperate feel on a half-empty dance floor, as if it were trying to send pulsating rays of frenzy into the still-sober crowd. They should just keep it dark until the wee hours, when it seemed perfectly normal. "I've always heard that a lot of prostitutes are lesbians. I don't know what to say, really. It's not that it bothers me that you have sex with men." Except it did.

"I don't have sex with men. I have sex with women, and they pay me for it."

Ryan continued to look at Miranda as the wheels rapidly spun in her brain. She looked over to where Val was dancing with Diane and saw an equally blank look on her friend's face. She looked back at Miranda and put a little more distance between them. "I don't pay to have sex. Don't see any reason to. Not that it's ever come up before."

"No, I don't imagine you have any trouble finding girls." Miranda kept her distance from Ryan, but ran her fingers through Ryan's thick hair and smiled. "But I can offer something that only the rare girl can that sleeps with you."

"And what would that be?" Ryan asked.

"Anything you want to do with no strings attached."

Ryan found her heart accelerating again as she imagined the

possibilities. But how could she reconcile herself to paying for sex? She wanted Miranda to want her just for her. The situation presented so many conflicting feelings that they essentially cancelled each other out. Walking away from Miranda was not the option she would select.

"How much?"

"Two hundred quid." Miranda smiled and kept the same open expression on her face. "I'm worth every tuppence."

"Jesus." Ryan fumbled a bit and smiled sheepishly. "I'm new at this, so I've got to ask. What does two hundred pounds get me, so to speak?"

"I promise you will not be unsatisfied. Do you have a flat nearby?"

Ryan signaled Val that she was leaving and wondered briefly whether Val was going to take the other woman up on her offer. Then she forgot about Val. By the time they arrived by cab at Ryan's nearby Bloomsbury flat, she was close to coming from Miranda's ministrations. The cabbie glanced into the rear view mirror several times before pulling over on Ryan's street. Ryan quickly paid the driver and led Miranda to the top floor of the Georgian building, pulling her in for a kiss as soon as the door was closed behind them.

"Pay first. Then no more has to be said about it. It's better that way," Miranda said.

"Fine. Why don't you get yourself sorted out, find the bathroom or whatever, and I'll be right back."

Ryan went into her study and found some cash and returned to her front room. Miranda had her coat off and her bag nearby, sitting perfectly composed on the sofa. She rose and came to Ryan, placing her hands on Ryan's hips and drawing them close into her own. Ryan slowly placed the cash in her hand as she leaned over and drew Miranda into a long and passionate kiss. Then she gently pushed her away and walked over to sit on the sofa where Miranda had just been. She was alarmed at how her heart began galloping each time she kissed Miranda. "Will you take off your clothes for me?"

"Of course." Miranda began to remove her clothing slowly, deliberately, in a practical manner that was sexier for its lack of coyness. She revealed to Ryan a beautifully proportioned, athletic body, full breasted but with slim hips and lean arms and legs. "What would you like now?"

Ryan stared at the woman before her and tried to think creatively, but she felt enveloped by a fog of arousal. She remembered that she was paying for the privilege of indulging herself, having her wishes catered to. There was no wooing necessary.

"I'd like you to touch yourself."

"While I stand here?"

"No, come lie on the sofa." Ryan slowly expelled her breath and rubbed her hands along her thighs, trying to calm herself, as Miranda lay against the arm of the sofa, her feet resting against Ryan. Her hands began to make their way down her body, first pausing to circle and play with her nipples, then moving slowly down to between her legs. Her left hand reached in to pull a lip back and her right began moving down, dipping in to capture some moisture, moving back to spread it around. Her fingers now moved over and around her clitoris, and they both moaned.

"Do you want me to come?" Miranda asked. "Because I can come for you, so easily."

"No. Not yet."

"You're in charge, darling. But I can't promise I won't come if I do this much longer."

"Just stick you finger in, two fingers, as far in as you can go."

Miranda did as she was told, and began to breathe more rapidly. "God, it feels good. Don't you want to be in here?"

"Soon. Come over here and kneel in front of me." Ryan had removed her belt and was pulling her trousers down, lifting her butt off the sofa and then kicking the pants off one leg. Miranda knelt in front of her and stared up at Ryan.

"All right," Ryan rasped. "Show me how good you are. Make me come." Miranda leaned over and began kissing around Ryan's belly, her inner thigh, inching her way closer to Ryan's core. Before she got there Ryan gently took hold of the hair on the back of Miranda's head and guided her mouth to her clitoris. "Right there. Use your tongue."

Ryan struggled to stay focused on Miranda's mouth moving against her, but she was almost instantly at the point of coming. Her head fell back against the sofa and she cried out as Miranda expertly worked her clitoris. Soon she was screaming as she came, holding Miranda's head against her, moving her hips frantically, without control. When she finally collapsed, barely conscious, she reached out and gently pulled Miranda forward so that she came up on the sofa and snuggled against her.

"You okay there, sailor?" Miranda asked, a smile in her voice as she burrowed in closer. "That sounded like a dangerously big orgasm."

"Yeah. I needed to get that out of the way. I couldn't think straight."

"Hmm. Sounds like you have plans for more."

"Oh, yes." Ryan raised her head and looked at Miranda. "You can stay longer, right?"

"I'm all yours."

They lay quietly and soon Ryan was busy thinking again. With other women she never had much trouble moving on to more lovemaking. With Miranda she was starting to feel paralyzed, as if she had to impress her with inventiveness. She wanted to impress her somehow.

"Have you ever strapped one on and fucked a girl?" Miranda asked. "Or wanted to?"

That is exactly what I want to do, Ryan thought. It's not inventive, but it's perfect. How did she know? "I don't have the equipment," she said.

"I do." Miranda rummaged around a bit in her bag and came up with a silk container. She drew from it a realistically shaped dildo and leather harness. Ryan felt her heart start to accelerate again as she reached to take it from Miranda. She stood and took Miranda by the hand, leading her to her bedroom.

"Pull the covers back and lie on the bed while I put this on." Ryan felt another surge of arousal as she watched Miranda follow her commands. She placed the dildo in the harness and pulled the contraption over her hips, tightening it so there was no play. "Now spread your legs for me so I can see you." Ryan climbed onto the bed as Miranda spread her legs and placed her hands along her inner thighs. Ryan thought her eyes looked a little glazed and she wondered for a moment how excited prostitutes actually got. Ryan lowered herself so that her face was between Miranda's legs and she started to kiss and suck and lick her in every conceivable way. Now there was no doubt of Miranda's arousal, for the physical evidence was plain. She was dripping wet and starting to writhe.

"I need you inside me. Please, hurry." Miranda was urging Ryan upward and over her. Ryan looked down, wondering if she'd survive the physical challenge. Her heart was pounding and she hadn't even entered her yet. Her clit was pounding as well, just above the base of the cock.

"Help me put it in," Ryan said as she began to lower herself, aiming toward Miranda as Miranda guided her in.

"Oh, god, god, god, god," Miranda said, moving her hips upward to take in more and more. Ryan moved her hips forward and stroked in, feeling the tip of her cock bump up against Miranda, the base bump up against her own clitoris. The feel of it, the sight of Miranda with her head thrown back and her mouth open, almost made her come. Slowly she pulled out, nearly all the way, and Miranda cried out and pulled Ryan back into her, crying out again as the length slid into her. Soon they found a rhythm and soon after that the rhythm grew faster. With each thrust Ryan felt more intensely connected to the woman below her, more intensely poised to explode. Ryan came first, shocked, screaming, and yet somehow able to keep stroking until Miranda came a few moments later. The collapse was utter. They neither moved nor said a word for long minutes.

Finally, Ryan stirred. "I loved that."

"Well, you're a natural. You were brilliant." Miranda smiled at Ryan and touched her hand to her cheek. "Does your girlfriend in the States appreciate how good you are?"

"I don't have a girlfriend."

"Really? How odd. You strike me as one who'd have a girlfriend."

Ryan was quiet a while longer and kept herself snuggled against Miranda, trying to figure out if she'd just been complimented or not. She looked at Miranda as she stretched the length of her quite spectacular body and then tried to stifle a yawn.

"Why don't I get you some tea? I can put something together to eat if you'd like."

"That's okay. I was going to have to go." Miranda moved out of Ryan's arms and swung her legs over the side of the bed. "You were lovely, darling. I hope our paths cross again sometime."

Ryan's hand reached over to touch Miranda. "May I call you?"

"I'll give you one of my cards. You mustn't give the number to anyone else. That isn't safe for me." Miranda had risen and was heading toward the other room. "I'll just bring that back to you." Ryan continued to lay curled up in bed, her body drained from the two powerful orgasms.

When Miranda returned to the bedroom she was dressed, with her coat on and bag in hand. She placed a business card on the nightstand and then leaned over to kiss Ryan.

"I think you forgot something," Ryan said, unbuckling the harness and handing it over.

"Ah, thanks very much. It wouldn't do to walk off without that," Miranda said, tucking everything into her bag. "You were fantastic. I hope you call me."

"Really?" Ryan tried not to show how very much she wished that were true.

"Really. Now, you just stay there and I'll see myself out. Goodbye, love."

And she was gone. Ryan drifted over to the window facing the street and watched as Miranda emerged from her building and headed toward Tottenham Court Road. She watched as Miranda pulled a cell phone out of her pocket and dialed, and she watched until Miranda turned the corner and could no longer be seen.

The phone rang several times before going into Diane's voicemail. Miranda spoke into the phone as she walked quickly down the street. "Diane, my sweet. Apparently you are still with your customer, while I'm quite finished with mine. I'm heading back to The Wine Bin since it's just gone midnight. I should have time for one more, which will make for quite a profitable night. Okay, love, see you back at the flat."

Miranda disconnected and picked up her pace as she slipped the phone back in her pocket.

ABOUT THE CONTRIBUTORS

JACQUELINE APPLEBEE is a black, bisexual British woman who breaks down barriers with smut. Jacqueline's stories have appeared in *Cleansheets*, *Iridescence: Sensuous Shades of Lesbian Erotica*, *Best Women's Erotica 2008*, *Best Lesbian Erotica 2008*, and *Ultimate Lesbian Erotica 2008*. She also has a paranormal novella that includes sex with ghosts! Jacqueline's Web site is at http://www.writing-in-shadows .co.uk.

CHARLOTTE DARE pens erotic adventures at various coffeehouses in Connecticut while eavesdropping on loud talkers seated nearby. Her fiction has appeared in *Tales of Travelrotica for Lesbians, Vol. 2*, *Ultimate Lesbian Erotica 2008*, *Wetter*, *Purple Panties*, and *Island Girls.* Visit her at www.myspace.com/charlotte_dare.

GENEVA KING (www.msgenevaking.com) has stories appearing in several anthologies, including: *Ultimate Lesbian Erotica 2006*, *Best Women's Erotica 2006*, *Ultimate Undies*, *Caramel Flava*, and *Travelrotica for Lesbians 1 & 2*. A transplant to Northern Maryland, she's constantly on the prowl for her next muse.

KIMBERLY LAFONTAINE lives in Texas and can often be found sitting by the Trinity River in Fort Worth with her laptop, hashing out the plot for her next book. Writing is her passion, her therapy, her hobby, and her favorite activity. LaFontaine has published three lesbian romance novels through Intaglio Publications: *Picking Up the Pace* (2005), *Preying on Generosity* (2007), and *Let It Shine* (2008). Feel free to contact her at kimberlylafontaine@yahoo.com.

MADLYN MARCH is the pseudonym of a journalist who has written for the *New York Post*, *Time Out New York*, *Self*, *Complete Woman*, AfterEllen.com, and many others. Her work has also appeared in the anthologies *First-Timers* and *Spanked: Red-Cheeked Erotica*. When not writing erotica, she can be found listening to old music or watching old movies.

CLAIRE MARTIN's erotica has appeared in *Erotic Interludes 4: Extreme Passions* (Bold Strokes Books, 2006) and *Erotic Interludes 5: Road Games* (2007). She lives in Chicago.

GILL MCKNIGHT lives and works between Ireland, the UK, and Greece. She has contributed short stories to the award-winning *Best Women's Erotica 2008* (Cleis Press), *Romantic Interludes:1* (Bold Stroke Books), and *Read These Lips: Openings.* Her debut novel, *Falling Star*, was published by Bold Stroke Books in July 2008, and will be followed by *Green-Eyed Monster* in December 2008.

GENEVA NIXON is a twenty-two-year-old college student residing in Texas. It has been her tireless goal to convey the erotic, sensual moments shared by two women in written form. Done stylishly, this can be a powerful mechanism in the art of sexual stimulation. To whoever reads her work, she hopes they find it to be exciting and honest.

Eroticist, environmentalist, and pastry enthusiast **GISELLE RENARDE** is a proud Canadian. She is the author of *Tangled Roots* and *Cunning Little Vixens* (eXcessica) and a short story contributor to numerous anthologies, including *Love Bites* (Torquere Press), *Tasting Her* (Cleis Press), *Coming Together: With Pride* (Phaze), and *Best Lesbian Love Stories 2009* (Alyson Books); her work is inspired by feminist ideology and the worlds of visual and performance art. Ms. Renarde lives across from a park with two bilingual cats who sleep on her head.

MIEL ROSE is a low-income, high-intensity queer femme. She grew up rurally in Vermont and still doesn't understand how to reconcile urban versus rural expressions of gender. She tends to write about girls who bear a striking resemblance to herself and the butches she wishes were in her bed. You can find her other stories in *Best Women's Erotica 2008, Best Lesbian Erotica 2008,* and the forthcoming *Tough Girls 2: More Down and Dirty Dyke Erotica* and *Best Lesbian Love Stories 2009*. "Love Letter" is, well, a love letter to butch/femme dynamics.

STEPHANIE ROSE is the pen name of Nikii Collier, an African-American lesbian erotica writer. Once a corporate attorney, she left the legal profession and became a full-time writer, and she is now happier than she has ever been before. She loves and adores smart, sexy women, and she is always ready to put those passions down on paper. She encourages women to always follow their dreams and to experience all the love and joy that life has to offer. For even more, please visit StephanieRoseHeat.com.

SANDRA ROTH is the pseudonym for a freelance writer with an MFA from The School of the Art Institute of Chicago. The author lives and works in Chicago. Sandra probably lives in LA. She seems like the type.

K. SONTZ is a young writer living in Brooklyn, New York. Sontz makes ends meet by working as a clerk in a bookstore but is currently pursuing a career in writing.

KISSA STARLING is a woman of many words. Her stories range from sweet to sizzling and everything in between. What started as a few words written in a diary has turned into a full-fledged writing career. Writing for Whiskey Creek Press Torrid and Red Rose Publishing is fun and interesting for her. She spends time each and every day dreaming up plots, researching settings, and dreaming up characters. Dare to experience the writing of this audacious author! Mrs. Starling spends most of her time with her family and pets in Georgia. Yoga, meditation, reading, reviewing, watching movies, and riding on the back of a motorcycle are just a few of her favorite pastimes. She also loves anything vintage and can't resist a sparkly, beaded purse. For more information, book covers, story blurbs, and the latest news, please visit www.kissastarling.com

DONNA GEORGE STOREY's erotic fiction has been published in over eighty journals and anthologies, including *Sexiest Soles*, *Dirty Girls*, *Spanked: Red-Cheeked Erotica*, *She's on Top*, *Best American Erotica 2006*, and the last five volumes of *Mammoth Book of Best New Erotica* and *Best Women's Erotica*. Her erotic novel *Amorous Woman* (Neon/Orion), a semiautobiographical tale of an American's steamy love affair with Japan, was released in the U.S. in 2008. Read more of her work at www.DonnaGeorgeStorey.com.

HEATHER TOWNE's writing credits include *Hustler Fantasies*, *Leg Sex*, *Newcummers*, *Naughty Neighbors*, *18eighteen*, *FRM*, *Forum*, *Scarlet*, and stories in the anthologies *Skin Deep 2*, *Mammoth Book of Women's Erotic Fantasies*, *Wicked Words*, *Nexus Confessions*, *Show & Tell*, *The Good Parts*, *Travelrotica 2*, and *Ultimate Lesbian Erotica 2005* and *2008*.

ANNA WATSON is an old-school femme living in the Boston area. She has stories in various anthologies, including *Best Lesbian Erotica 2007, 2008, 2009*, as well as *Fantasy: Untrue Stories of Lesbian Passion*. She writes for Custom Erotica Source as Cate Shea, and keeps an intermittent blog on queertoday. She feels that there is not nearly enough butch/femme erotica out there and is doing her best to remedy the situation.

LARA ZIELINSKY, using the nom de plume LZClotho for online Xena and Voyager fanfiction, resides in Orlando, Florida, home of Mickey Mouse. Her first published novel, *Turning Point*, published by P.D. Publishing, Inc., won the 2007 Lesbian Fiction Readers Choice Award and was a finalist for the 2008 Golden Crown Literary Society Award. Previously she has had stories published in various lesbian short story anthologies. Her Web site is www.lzfiction.net